# Charred

Lesley Moody

# ACKNOWLEDGMENTS

Thank you to Adam, Celeste, Shannon, Shawna, Jason, & Kajal,
who read, and helped refine my work.

# WHY DON'T YOU JUST...

"Everyone, back! Give them room!" Mr. Hammond punctuated each word as his voice boomed above the crowd. Other teachers pushed students back as they inched closer, trying to get a look at the girl lying motionless in the middle of the road.

"I didn't see her. She ran out of nowhere." The driver of the car was frantic. He paced back and forth, wringing his hands, as he looked from his children, already belted into the back seat of the car, to the girl lying on the ground. His head shook from side to side in disbelief.

Students pushed in closer, curious about the scene that had exploded only minutes earlier. One young girl, however, stood at the back of the crowd, muttering to herself.

"It's not my fault. She's crazy. It's not my fault."

The paramedics arrived within minutes, and Mr. Hammond assumed his position in the human barrier between the sea of middle school students and Alex.

"Is she dead?" One girl's voice rose above the hundreds of whispers that filled the schoolyard.

"I think she's unconscious," another answered. The crowd became louder as each second passed, and each person weighed in with their opinion.

"I've never seen a dead person." The whispers grew to a soft rumble.

"Who is it?"

"The crazy girl I think."

"Did she run out in front of the car on purpose?" Polite whispers soon disappeared. Accusations and predictions rocketed around the yard.

"Probably."

"Suicide?"

"That's terrible."

"THAT will be quite enough!" bellowed Mr. Hammond. "Everyone back up! Get on your buses! Start walking home! There is nothing left to see here!" Of course, he was entirely wrong. There was plenty to see as the paramedics stabilized Alex's head, checked her vital signs. Alex's hand flopped off the edge of the gurney as it rattled to standing position, causing one of the girls to scream.

"O-M-G, she is totally dead!" The shriek echoed across the yard.

Tasha, still muttering to herself, backed away from the churning group. Regardless of its mussed state, her dyed black hair fell perfectly around her perfectly proportioned face. The slightest chin quiver betrayed her tough appearance. Her black skirt fit just tight enough to cause her father grief, and her matching tank top covering just enough skin to avoid issues with the teachers. The addition of crimson lipstick, nail polish, and a few forbidden piercings over the past few years, had transformed her from a preppy cheerleader to a venomous spider. Despite her unexplained transformation, her entourage was stuck firmly in her web of influence.

Three female onlookers stared at her in horror. They were the only other students not fixated on the flashing lights and EMTs, their outfits matched the style clearly outlined by their Queen. Their hair, also masterfully coiffed, cascaded in tussled strands around their shoulders. Eyes wide, mouths open, they waited for a response from their leader. Seeing judgment creeping over their faces woke Tasha from her trance. Her chin jerked upward, allowing her to look down her nose at her entourage, even though she was the shortest of the group.

"You don't honestly think we had anything to do with this?" She rolled her eyes and reverted to her usual mannerisms. Her ebony hair flipped off her shoulder as she pulled a compact out of her small purse. Slowly and deliberately, she touched up her lips and straightened the chain that ran from her fake nose ring to her ear. "We all know Alex was crazy. She was probably planning this for months."

One after the other, each of the girls let out their breath they had not realized they were holding. Their shoulders relaxed, and they

4

tossed their hair, mirroring their mentor. Of course, this wasn't their fault. They didn't push Alex in front of that car, they told themselves. For all they knew, she meant to run in front of the car.

Minutes earlier, the scene had been a typical afternoon at Scarblough Junior High. Classes had finished for the day, and a whole hive of students swarmed into the schoolyard to wait for rides, catch buses and plan their weekends. The week had been hot, summer was almost here, and everyone was more excited than usual for school to end. Giggles and screams filled the air as boys and girls yelled their plans and friendly jibes across the yard.

Alex walked, as per usual, with her head down, counting the tiles on the hallway floor until she reached the door. A weight lifted off her shoulders as she pushed through the exterior door of the school. Only fifty more meters and she'd be free for another day. The second she stepped out into the hot sun, pain exploded across her forehead. With her head down, she hadn't noticed their trap, a thick branch, held across the door at head height. Two boys in hysterics stood over her, rejoicing in their flawlessly executed prank. Her slight frame staggered back, and the books she had been carrying flew in every direction.

"Look, boys," came the snickering voice of Tasha Winham from the bottom of the stone steps, "she bounces." The entire group burst out laughing, attracting a few snickers from passing students.

Alex rubbed her head and began furiously gathering all her belongings. The blurred lines of the concrete glared up at her as her head throbbed. The contents of her bag spilled out, showering the steps with papers and books. She reached for the latest book she had borrowed from her father's library, a copy of Ender's Game, but it flew across the landing and down the steps along with the notebook she had taken off his desk. Her hand rested on the giant foot that took its place.

"Beep Boop, Beep Boop." Mark towered over most students, with broad shoulders and a muscular build. His buzzed hair and chiseled jawline gave him a tough and intimidating look, and his piercing blue eyes seemed to glare with malice. He poked at her on the ground. "I can't get this one to work, I think its defective." Chocolate brown hair fell across Alex's face. She was grateful for it, as it hid the burning tears that now welled up. Her blood boiled with anger and sadness simultaneously, and she felt the urge to fight back and disappear from existence at the same time. She wasn't surprised that she had been singled out. Alex had never tried to conform, but the hurtful words were like a never-ending hailstorm, making her feel small and alone. She had complained to her mother once but was only greeted with, "It will all be over soon. You'll see. None of it matters after you're done school. Just ignore them and they'll stop." What a load of crap.

Their latest target was her love of science fiction. Since Alex lost her father, she had begun to spend more time in his home office, reading his books, and exploring his passions. She had taken to reading through his old idea journals, reading about bioengineering, waste disposal, and complex alternative energy ideas that at this point in her life she had no chance of understanding. Still, knowing the words and drawings had been written by him comforted her. She had always loved reading, and preferred books to people, but it seemed like her new interests were one more bar in the battery that charged their disdain.

"Well, well, what do we have here." She looked up to see Tasha lifting the idea book from the sidewalk. Alex's heart stopped momentarily as Tasha stopped to read the cover of the journal.

"Trying to get extra credit?" She laughed and carelessly chucked the book back at Alex, hitting her in the chest. Alex was so relieved she hardly noticed the pain of the impact. Instead, the perfectly manicured hand picked up the novel and started thumbing through it.

"Don't touch that!" Alex's voice thundered across the front lawn of the school, momentarily stopping everyone in earshot.

"Touchy." Tasha laughed; her followers snickered like the good little swarm they were expected to be.

Alex shot up and lunged down the stairs toward the group. Stumbling forward on the last step, she desperately reached for the book. Seconds before she made contact, the tome sailed over her head and landed in sausage-like hands at the top of the stairs. Mark, still next to her bag on the top step, kicked it and the rest of the contents down the steps toward her with more force than was necessary then returned his attention to the book.

"Oh, this part looks good." Mark laughed and tore out a few pages from the middle and tossed them toward Alex. The book then sailed to another boy standing nearby.

"Oh yes, terribly interesting." the other boy snickered, "I've been looking for some new things to read. He spread it open, and a chunk was ripped from the middle.

The game proceeded for what seemed like a lifetime but was, in fact, only a few minutes. The pages fluttered to the ground, half torn, mixed, and stepped on. Alex gathered what she could, eyes stinging before running as fast as she could away from the crowd.

"Can't take a joke?" Tasha yelled after her, cackling laughter echoing in Alex's ears.

Seconds later, everything went black.

# THIS MUST BE...

The ground beneath her was cold and damp. She felt around, expecting concrete, but found only soft organic material. The phone she kept in her back pocket jabbed her lower back as the sounds of the schoolyard faded away, replaced by bird songs. A distant hum, which she could not identify, hovered in the air. She concluded that the sunny day had changed to overcast, as the sun no longer turned the inside of her eyelids bright red. It was as if a shadow had rolled over everything. Alex debated whether to open her eyes as she felt the grass beneath her, or at least what she thought must be grass. Like so many days when she woke, the feeling that the world would be better off if she kept her eyes closed for good pressed in on her. A throbbing rose in her head, thundering each heartbeat and drowning out what few noises surrounded her. The only sound remaining was the distant humming that grew louder every minute.

After a few minutes of contemplation, she gave in to her curiosity and let the new surroundings pour in. Her eyes were greeted by a foreboding gray sky. Turning to her right, she could see a great forest of trees, running in a perfectly straight line along the grassy ditch she lay in. Turning her head left, she saw a cobbled road bordered on the other side by an equally enchanting forest. Alex's heart skipped a beat as she realized she wasn't anywhere near her school or any place she recognized. The tickling sensation of eight tiny legs working their way up her arm had her sitting bolt upright in seconds. She slapped her arm, brushing frantically at the tiny harmless spider that had pushed her from relaxed curiosity to a flailing ninja with little effort. Once she had calmed slightly, she steadied herself against the sudden rush of blood to her head. Apparently, she was dreaming, but she couldn't remember going

8

home, let alone falling asleep. Part of her wondered why the eight-legged nightmare hadn't roused her as she rubbed the throbbing ache in the back of her head, and squinted her eyes, desperately trying to recall the past moments, with no success. The road appeared to go several kilometers before ending at what Alex assumed must be a city. There were no sprawling suburbs, or miles of rolling residential streets, however. It was too far to make out many details, but she could see a grand central building atop a hill. Squinting further, she could make out a circular web of roads and buildings surrounding it, giving the entire city a disc-shape appearance as if it had been walled in. Some of the buildings glistened in the sun, but the further away from the central building, the duller the buildings appeared. The longer she stared, the louder the humming became.

What is that?! She pressed her temples in response, willing it to stop, but the noise endured.

The allure of the forest called to her. If this was a dream, she would rather walk through an enchanted forest than along an abandoned road, no matter how enticing the shining city on the hill might be. Shrugging, she headed toward the woods. The shock that knocked her back was more of a tingle than pain, but she found herself flat on her back once again. The entire forest in front of her had turned into a greenish blue cascade of waves for a few seconds as she tumbled. Moments later, the scene in front of her returned to its original state. How could there be an invisible wall in the middle of her dream? She had certainly encountered them in video games, and perhaps this was a projection of that but weren't dreams supposed to be about what she wanted to do? The trees beyond looked exactly as they had before, only, now that she was analyzing more closely, she didn't smell the typical freshness that usually accompanied a forest. In fact, the air was stale and almost void of scent. She could barely smell the odor of the grass beneath her and chalked it up to dream mechanics.

Looking down, she inspected the grass. It looked like grass.

She breathed in deeply. It faintly smelled like grass, and it even almost felt like grass. The more she ran her fingers through it, the more she realized it was made from a polymer substance. Standing, she moved toward the invisible wall that had seconds before prevented her exploration. Extending her hand, she stopped when she felt resistance and let the continual pleasant tingling make its way up her arm. The trees beyond once again blurred into a million tiny, pixelated waves. Looking up, she could see the trees stretched toward the sky for at least a hundred meters. While they looked completely three-dimensional, clear, and real, not one of them had branches that cascaded over the invisible surface that locked them in.

The humming grew unbearably loud. Whirling around, she scanned the horizon to identify its source. Her eyes grew large as she took in the sight in front of her. Stopped on the road was a horse and carriage. The carriage was outlined in gold patterns of leaves and vines and reminded her of something she had seen in a Cinderella movie. The walls of the preposterous vehicle were made of matte silver chrome. Instead of wheels, however, the carriage appeared to hover above the ground. The words Anti-gravity Electromagnetic Field Study popped into her head, and she thought that perhaps she should stop reading her father's idea books before bedtime.

The air under the carriage was a distorted blur. Pulling the wagon was an enormous mechanical horse. Its entire body was made of cogs and gears, and its legs were a mess of wires and hydraulics. Blue glowing tubes ran out of its neck, cascading like a mane until they disappeared back into the side of the machine. It was the oddest, and most beautiful thing Alex had seen in her entire life.

The horse jerked its head up and down, pulling on its reins, waiting for its next directive. As it pawed the ground, a slim humanoid shape, also completely mechanical, calmed it. The artificial chauffeur wore a black velvet coat adorned with lace around its collar and cuffs. It didn't look at her or acknowledge her. Stoically, both horse and driver seemed to await a command from whomever, or whatever, was in the carriage.

The windows of the carriage were opaque, preventing her from satisfying her curiosity. She stood there, mouth open, wondering at the new characters she had dreamed up. As the carriage settled, the humming faded, and the vehicle slowly lowered to the ground behind the horse. Once it reached its final resting place, on the cobbles below, the audible world was once again bearable. The sound of birds chirping once more filled the air, and Alex wondered if there was a forest beyond the wall after all.

Her pondering was cut short as the door of the carriage hissed open, revealing a cushioned grey and gold interior. There was still no sign of its inhabitant, but a cheerful female voice called to her from within.

# ACTUALLY, IT'S...

"Well don't just stand there gawking my dear, come and introduce yourself properly." The statement was half request and half order. Alex was immediately self-conscious and began adjusting her t-shirt and hair as she slowly madeXXX her way toward the carriage. A set of grey velvet boots with black pearl buttons up the side became visible as she approached. The stranger slowly became visible the closer Alex got to the strange vehicle. Even in a sitting position, Alex could tell that the woman's dress was much shorter at the front than back, allowing for a full view of her knee-high boots. Its length didn't stop it from being frilly and overbearing. Around the woman's slender legs swam yards of black tulle. The sheer fabric was layered with grey silk embroidered with crimson red spades that traveled up the bodice. The layers were gathered forming ruffles at the side of the skirt, which disappeared into what Alex assumed was a bustle tucked behind.

The woman's torso was encased in a corset that stopped just under her breasts, and the neckline of the dress revealed a little more of the woman than Alex wished to observe. The sleeves continued off the shoulder and snuggly down the woman's arms until it reached her biceps where it fanned out once again, mirroring the short front and long back of her skirt. Despite its yards of tulle, the dress was glorious and reminded Alex of the gothic Victorian style she had seen while surfing the web.

The woman's face and hair were equally overdone, and her plastered smile made the whole ensemble seem like a parody. Platinum blonde hair spread out in awkward and deliberate spikes to form a peacock like fan at the back of her head. The rest of her hair was pulled back into several neat braids that were pinned tightly to reveal the woman's slender neckline. She wore crimson lipstick and dark eyeliner, reminding Alex of her band of tormentors back home. For a moment she fought back tears before deciding to focus on the absurdity of the woman now smiling at her from the carriage. Shaking her head clear, she finished her approach.

The ridiculousness of the woman was compounded once Alex arrived in front of the open door. The woman's eyes reminded Alex of a Japanese anime, and Alex was forced to stifle a giggle as she reached the side of the carriage. She wasn't prone to laughing at others since she had been the subject of ridicule many times, but the hilarity of the situation proved to be too much for her. The broad smile that had been painted across the woman's face disappeared in a flash, her teeth vanished behind her thick red lips, and the lines between her eyebrows grew grave and rigid. The look only lasted a few seconds before she shook her head and once again plastered a smile across her face as if it were a fashion accessory.

"Well, hello my dear. Surely you didn't intend to walk all the way to Thetis. Perhaps you would allow me to assist you?" Despite the woman's clear attempt at cheerfulness, her voice was weighty.

"Uh... actually... I'm taking a stroll through the forest." She pointed with her thumb over her shoulder. Through the carriage window on the other side of the road, she could see that it no longer had a thick lush row of trees. In their place was a flock of sheep, fenced in by moss-covered stone walls. Alex crinkled her forehead. Holding up a finger she turned abruptly and walked to the back of the carriage. The stranger inside gasped then harrumphed.

"What the actual..." Alex didn't finish the sentence as she peered around the other side of the carriage. The scene looked once again like it had when she first awoke. Thick trees with lush foliage lined the ditch. She looked from side to side, taking in the entire situation. The stranger made a show of clearing her voice. Alex returned to the door of the carriage, and the scene full of sheep disappeared.

"Wait..." Alex raised an eyebrow and cocked her head, "screens?"

Just when she thought the woman's smile could get no bigger, it spread even further, past the edges of her teeth, she wasn't sure she had seen a human's mouth reach such lengths.

"It appears we have a newcomer to Wonderland, my pet." The woman didn't take her eyes off Alex. After a quick scan of the compartment, Alex couldn't make out who the woman might be talking to; driver and horse perhaps?

"Wonderland?" Alex was starting to understand where her dream was coming from and decided to roll with it, secretly vowing to write it all down when she woke. After a few moments pause, the woman continued. "Please, come rest your legs, the forest is no place for a young girl to wander alone."

Alex took one last look over her shoulder toward the invisible wall behind her and was met instead with an up-close view of the robot driver's velvet coat. She jumped back, wondering how he could have so silently positioned himself without her noticing, and her heart thundered as he lifted her into the carriage with little effort. The cushion on the adjacent seat was as soft as it looked, and she sank deeper than she had anticipated.

It puffed up and embraced her legs as she sat. Oddly enough, the seat on the other side of the compartment didn't seem to hug the woman's legs in the same fashion. Maybe the girls at school were right, and she had put on a few too many pounds. Self-consciously, she felt her stomach. Her legs were almost entirely covered by fabric and padding. The cushion behind her, however, was more rigid, so she was able to sit up straight.

As she positioned herself comfortably, the carriage rose, and the humming resumed. The woman snapped her fingers, and the door to the carriage closed. Silence enveloped them. If only her noise cancelling worked this well. Once they were moving, Alex had time to survey the compartment. She could pick out decorative touches that reminded her of a Victorian coach. The gold leaves and vines that adorned the exterior continued inside, outlining each window. Three screens covered each side, and the only window provided a view of where they had been. Through it, she could see the road once again flanked by trees rising high into the sky. On the carriage screens, the scene had changed to a tropical rainforest. The picture was clearer than any television on earth, and she felt as if she was seeing living vegetation, solid enough to touch. It was as if on this world, Wonderland as the woman called it, they had created a realistic virtual environment that could be projected on a screen in front of you.

Alex could resist no longer, and she reached out to touch the screen. Similar to the invisible wall at the side of the road, a pixelated wave cascaded across the surface, originating from the spot she touched. The tingling that ran down her arm was much less intense than it had been outside, but she could feel the faint energy signal just the same. When she removed her hand, the waves disappeared. Thinking back to the invisible wall on the side of the road, she wondered what lay beyond the barrier.

"Terrible, isn't it? I'd love to get it replaced, but who wants to walk around wearing those ridiculous glasses? No, as you can see," the woman who had been quietly observing her up to this point motioned with her hand at the carriage around them. "I have an appreciation for the finer, more cultured, things this world has to offer. Would you like a spot of tea?"

Out of the floor between them a solid black stone platform rose and stopped at table height. Its sides had been covered in the same gold leaf pattern as the rest of the delicate features in the carriage.

"Tea. Earl Grey. Hot!" the woman smiled as she gave the order, her eyes bulging wider than ever.

The reference wasn't lost on Alex. She thought back to the many times she had watched Star Trek with her father before the accident. She would snuggle up under his arm, and together they would go where no man... or woman, he would remind her... had gone before. It was her father that had given her a passion for everything science fiction. In fact, she concluded that he would have loved Wonderland. A vision of him flashed in her mind. He was standing in a stark white room, a look of pleading on his face. He beckoned for her to come closer, and his lips moved, but she couldn't hear his words. The vision only lasted a few seconds before she was brought back to her current reality.

Since his death during the previous school year, her mother worked longer hours to compensate for the reduced income. Alex was left on her own to deal with everything life had to throw at her. Things had been rocky for the few months before the respite of summer saved her from the awkward stares and unvoiced questions. She took the opportunity to retreat into her books, video games, and every sci-fi movie and series she could get her hands on. That's when she found the first idea book tucked beside a copy of Dune. It was as if her father had hidden them for her like Easter Eggs.

When September rolled around again, she didn't have many friends, or any she would call more than acquaintances, so she easily managed to keep most of her deepest feelings from anyone at school. Of course, her mother had alerted the principal that Alex had "retreated into her grief", so the teachers were annoyingly more 'delicate' with her than any of the other students. This didn't go unnoticed by Tasha and her gang, who had, up until that point, had other people to traumatize.

She had imagined that things would get back to normal upon her return. Homerooms had shifted, however, placing her directly across the aisle from Tasha. That's when the relentless jibes started. At first, Alex held her head up high, pushing aside what they said, trying to be confident in herself, as the school programs had always nagged her to do.

Alex was jarred out of her daydream as two steaming cups of tea in pink and gold china suddenly appeared on the table in front of them. A matching pot and plate of biscuits accompanied them. The liquid in the cup was motionless, and Alex noticed for the first time that the hover carriage seemed motionless even though she could clearly see the road moving behind them. As if reading her mind the woman's voice broke the silence.

"It is amazing how smooth a ride can get when you take the wheels away." She picked up her teacup and sipped, leaving a red smudge on the edge. Alex did the same. The tea tasted delightful. It was sweeter than any tea she had ever tasted, and it warmed her insides as it traveled down through her chest.

"Where am I?" Alex found her voice for the first time since stepping into the carriage. The woman just stared at her analytically, observing her wonder. She seemed utterly fascinated and delighted by Alex's lack of knowledge.

"Well, right now you are in one of the most significant carriages in Wonderland, heading to the central city of Thetis. I'm sure we've been over this." The woman kept her cheerful disposition, her smile still plastered into position. In fact, it made Alex very uncomfortable. She had flash visions of attacking clowns, and psychotic dolls and had no desire for her dream to go in that direction. Although, it would almost certainly ensure that she would wake up.

"Riiiiiight," Alex raised her eyebrows questioningly at the woman. "I'm very grateful to have the privilege of being with such an important figure... Ms...?" Alex couldn't hold back her patronizing tone. The woman lost some of her smile, which seemed more frightening than when it was frozen to her face, and Alex quickly added, "Pardon my ignorance. As you observed, I'm... new to these parts."

The edges of the woman's lips slingshot back into position, "Of course dear. I'm Ciara Philonious Eugine, a lady in waiting to the Queen." Alex hadn't imagined that the woman could become any puffier, but her chest filled as she tilted her chin upward as if awaiting applause.

"Mmm," was all Alex could muster, her eyebrows once again raised toward her hairline. She could stifle her laughter no longer. The entire situation was ridiculous. She was in Wonderland, in a hover carriage filled with virtual technology, sitting across from a woman who looked like a frilly Goth girl, who claimed to be a lady in waiting to the Queen. The next thing she expected was to hear that the Queen was fond of roses and would chop off your head in an instant if you disobeyed. She wasn't sure what possessed her to dream about one of her childhood tales, but she could, at least, find the humour in it.

Based on her expression, Ciara didn't find the situation as hilarious. In fact, the plastered smile turned into a ferocious glare. Her teeth clenched together, the bright white contrasting against her blood red lips. This was usually the part of the movie when a chainsaw was produced, and Alex sobered slightly. The woman spoke through clenched teeth.

"I would think you would be grateful for my hospitality. I suppose I shouldn't be surprised. I've never found a grateful pet yet."

"Wait... what?" As the question left her lips, the puffy cushions surrounding her legs became stiff. The more she squirmed, the harder it became to move. She pulled at the cushion's fabric, but it appeared to grow larger and fuller with each tug until it fully enclosed her legs in a tight grip. Alex's mouth went dry, and she tasted bitterness where the sweetness of the tea's aftertaste had once been. All at once, the sounds of the carriage, the mechanical tromping of the horse hooves in front of them, and the buzz of the screens surrounding them became apparent. Every one of Alex's senses was alight with sensation.

"Just relax," the woman's patronizing voice rang out. "It will all be over a lot sooner if you don't struggle." Her pale arm, surrounded by ruffles rose to a gold cord that dangled beside her.

Now would be a good time to wake up, Alex thought. Trying to hurry the process along, she pinched her leg, which tingled under the pressure of her restraints. As the woman pulled the cord, a small door opened above Alex's head and bright light enveloped her. There was a beeping as red lasers flashed across her skin, scanning her. She continued to struggle, trying desperately to free herself. After about five minutes of zero progress, she gave up, going slack under her own exhaustion. The beeping that filled the air had given a few final peeps before she felt a wave of sensation, like a million tiny brushes tickling her skin at the same time. She watched as her legs grew smaller under the restraints, the rest of her body following suit. Her body shrunk until it fit entirely into the impression of the hardened cushion where she had once been imprisoned. She guessed that she was now no larger than a mouse.

Ciara smirked down at her, as she attempted to crawl across the cushion, but before she reached the edge, she was lifted by her collar and was moved through the air. Ciara pressed another button, disguised as a gold leaf, on the side of the compartment. A door the size of a glove box slid open, revealing a half-dozen additional miniature captives in various states of boredom, anger, and despair. A few huddled in the corner, half asleep or half alive, Alex had trouble telling. Another tall slim man with disheveled hair and moth-eaten clothing that seemed to be out of a medieval story book yelled and screamed, veins popping, pacing across the front of the empty compartment, making no attempt to escape, but clearly upset at his predicament. Two young girls, the smallest of the bunch, and possibly sisters, huddled together off to one side. The first girl, seemingly between 8 and 10 years of age, had a round cherubic face, curly red hair and two messy pigtails. Her rosy cheeks were stained with tears as another girl, slightly taller with a similarly round face and matching red locks pulled into a tight bun, comforted her. Only one interested captive, a rogue like air about her, seemed to be watching intently. A look of part concern, part curiosity, and one hundred percent amusement adorned her face. Vibrant purple and pink striped hair flowed around a petite face, piercing green eyes squinted their interest, and a mysterious grin that seemed to stretch wider than should be possible.

Alex kicked and poked at Ciara's hands, but her efforts had little impact. In an instant, Alex was flying toward the open compartment. She felt a slight tingle of electricity as she entered the box and landed with a thud. A white-hot pain she'd never felt before shot through her shoulder. Looking down, she saw her arm dangling at her side. As she attempted to push herself up, another excruciating pain gripped her. A few seconds later, the compartment door slid shut and the inky darkness spread over them.

Soft and nimble hands touched her leg.

"NO!" Alex yelled frantically as she kicked outward toward her attacker. "Get away from me." Then to herself she mumbled. "This is a dream. I need to wake up. Why won't I wake up?" She tried to push, but each movement sent new waves of pain throughout her entire torso.

"I assure you; this is not a dream." The voice of a young girl answered her back. It was assertive, yet non-aggressive. "If you'll allow me, I need to set your shoulder." A light came on, and the space around them illuminated. Looking up, she saw the purple and pink hair before noticing anything else. Closer now, she could see that the girl's hair was cropped into a short bob. The worn leather jacket she wore matched her sturdy well-used pants. It was what Alex had imagined a thief in a party of adventures might look like. She was young, but her eyes showed wisdom beyond her years.

"My names Ches" The girl reached forward and touched Alex's arm softly. The two young girls had moved forward to get a view; both faces now dry. In what Alex assumed was an attempt to distract her, Ches continued. "This is Tilly and Tully, just met them myself not that long ago, and you are?"

"Uh... Alex...." She looked back and forth between the crowd that was gathering around her. "Why does it hurt so much, dreams aren't supposed to hurt so much?" The faces were a daze as she scanned them trying to catch her barring's.

"Again, I'm not sure what you're going on about, but she's watching us... and listening." As if urging her to silence, Ches nodded to the closed compartment door and was silent for the next few minutes as she adjusted Alex into position.

"Ready for this?" Without waiting for a response, Ches placed one hand on Alex's shoulder and the other on her elbow. In one swift movement, Alex felt her arm being jammed back into place. The sensation felt more like her arm was being ripped away than being put back. Alex tried to remain present, but the last thing she thought before passing out was. Finally, I can wake up.

# OUT OF THE DRAWER

The hospital room whirred with noise. Beeping from the monitor, hissing from an oxygen tank, and shuffling from the nurses and doctors in the hallway made an almost harmonic rhythm. Mrs. Henderson sat staring at her daughter, eyes glazed. She had been in the city, in the middle of a mediation, when she got the call that Alex had been struck. She had walked out with no explanation, acknowledgment, or even goodbye. Her zombie-like state was enough to alert any doomsday theorist if they had seen her, but no one in her office attempted to stop her. In fact, most of them didn't even look up from the conference table. The negotiation was going poorly anyway, and after her strange disappearance, the deal was likely off the table entirely.

The flight was short, and luckily there had been one leaving immediately. A few hours had gone by since she placed herself in the uncomfortable visitor's chair beside Alex. About an hour ago, the doctors had set her daughter's dislocated shoulder. The injury was not present when Alex arrived. Of course, Mrs. Henderson knew that it was improbable for the injury to simply manifest, but the hospital claimed that her daughter's shoulder just magically popped out of the socket. Too tired to fight at the moment, she stared at the wall, counting the number of lines on the outdated wallpaper.

All she wanted was for someone to fill her in on the details. She wanted news, any news, about Alex's condition. Surely there must be something known. Why had they left her waiting so long? If she weren't so worried about the young girl lying in front of her, she would already be blazing through the halls, searching for the doctor in charge. She stroked the hair along Alex's temple and sang *Can't Help Falling in Love*, the only song that used to quiet Alex as John rocked her to sleep at night.

Another pang caught in Mrs. Henderson's throat as she remembered her late husband. She had lost him only eighteen months ago; she couldn't lose her daughter too. It had been everything she could do to keep things together after his mission failure. He had been testing new energy sources on behalf of the Canadian Space Agency at a NASA facility in Florida when a power surge overloaded. The clean room he was in was filled with electrical waves, and the three scientists in the room had died instantly, so they told her. Partly to deal with her grief, and partly to make ends meet, she had thrust herself into her work.

"Mrs. Henderson?" The voice came from the door, startling her from mourning. As she looked up, she saw a young doctor. Short, stylish, cropped hair complimented his olive skin and chiseled chin. She had to keep her eyes from rolling as she was reminded of the silly medical dramas she had a habit of watching but was relieved that someone was finally here to see her.

"Call me Barb." She welcomed him into the room, turning to face him. His own badge read Dr. Fernandez, but he didn't bother to introduce himself.

"Will Mr. Henderson be joining us?"

"No," was all she said, not wishing to see the look of pity that usually crossed people's faces when she told them of his passing.

"Very well. Mrs. Henderson... Barb... Alex is a unique case." He stopped, waiting for her to acknowledge, but she just stared at him, face blank, waiting. He cleared his throat. "You see, we've never seen anything quite like this in a patient with a state of prolonged unconsciousness."

"You mean... she's in a coma?" Her eyes widened and horror spread across her face.

The doctor hesitated, "That's not exactly the term we would use, but if it is easier for you to understand, then yes, we can use the term coma. Has no one been in to see you yet?"

"No. I've been waiting here for days."

"I apologize Mrs. H... Barb, let me start from the beginning." He lifted his leg and placed his hip on the other bed in the room, though he didn't lower his clipboard or look directly into Barb's eyes.

"Your daughter was hit by a car outside the school yard. The driver wasn't going very fast, and the injuries were quite minimal. There didn't even seem to be any head trauma. By all accounts she should have bounced back up at the site of the accident. Instead, she has been in a state of prolonged un... a coma, since she arrived." Horror turned to confusion as Barb listened, not daring to interrupt, "In fact, the car barely bumped her. From onlooker comments to police on the scene, we think she may even have lost consciousness before the vehicle made contact, and the driver happened to be in the wrong place at the wrong time. Was your daughter having any troubles?"

"What do you mean troubles?" Barb stared at him confused.

"Drugs? Partying? Alcohol? The tox screens came back negative, but we have to rule everything out." He looked up at her for the first time, a look of accusation firmly planted on his face.

"No! Absolutely not. I mean... I don't think so. I've been busy. Not too busy for my daughter of course, but work..." Barb let herself trail off. Had she really been doing everything she could for her daughter?

"This is impossible," Barb lashed out. "Why would someone just fall into a coma?"

"That's the question we're trying to answer. Sometimes in severely depressed patients, we see the chemicals in the brain interact negatively with their medications. That's why we need to know if Alex was on any medication? Experimenting with any drugs? Could she have taken anything?"

"Depression? Alex wasn't depressed. She was a perfectly normal teenager. Sure, her life wasn't perfect, but she was quiet and kept to herself. There must be...." Barb stopped short as the doctor raised his clipboard and wrote something.

"According to her medical records, Alex visited the clinic and was prescribed antidepressants about four months ago. Were you unaware of your daughter's condition?" The doctor's indifferent attitude infuriated Barb. How could Alex have been prescribed anything without her knowing?

"This is a mistake. I would have known. How could she get antidepressants without my permission?" Her tone was more accusatory than she had wanted it to be.

"It says here that you signed the necessary forms." He flipped through some papers on his clipboard, and she was sure that his tone was, in fact, accusatory.

"I am not a bad parent. I'm not one of those parents that forget they have a child. I knew what Alex was doing and where she was. She was an honor student. She came home every night! I never had to worry about her! She was perfectly happy! I don't know what you're implying here but…" Barb's disbelief at her own negligence filled her with guilt, and her agitation grew with each statement. How had she blindly signed a form for a prescription? Was she really that oblivious?

"Mrs. Henderson, no one is implying anything. We're just trying to make the proper diagnosis. Perhaps Alex was suffering more than she let on. Were there any serious incidents in the past few years?"

Barb hesitated. "Her father died eighteen months ago, but she's been fine. She's never complained. She hasn't even cried since the funeral. It's been much harder for me than for her."

"Was she talking to anyone about the loss?"

Barb just stared in disbelief. She hadn't thought to get any counselor for Alex, but clearly someone had prescribed medicine for her. Perhaps Alex was just putting on a happy face.. This was her fault!

"Were there any issues at school?" The doctor continued down what sounded like a checklist.

"Oh…uh…" Barb snapped out of her own contemplation, "No, I don't think so. Maybe… I had a phone call last week. I haven't had the chance…" Fresh tears began to well up in Barb's eyes. She had been so wrapped up in her own life that she had forgotten to check in with her own daughter. The school *had* called, and she was supposed to get back to them with an appointment time. She had assumed it was grade related, that Alex had let her grades slip. Since she had always been an exemplary student, Barb had shrugged it off, giving Alex some deserved leeway.

"There is one more question. Have you noticed anything, found anything at home, that might suggest that Alex was contemplating suicide?" The question came out so compassionless that it hit her straight in the chest like a gunshot. Barb took a sharp intake of breath. It took every ounce of energy she had to stop from pouncing on the man.

"I only ask because one of the teachers relayed that rumors were spreading after the accident. Of course, it could be child fantasy and storytelling so it's likely nothing, but I must ask."

Barb thought back, scouring the house with her mind, Alex's room, every situation she could remember, and every interaction she could think of over the past few months with her daughter. Sadly, there weren't that many. She just shook her head.

"Perhaps I should come back after you've had a chance to digest all of this." He turned to go.

"No. I've been waiting long enough, please… You said she was a unique case?" Reluctantly the doctor turned around and took a spot on the opposite side of Alex's bed. He pointed to a black screen with various waves moving across it.

"We performed an EEG. This is Alex's brain activity." He showed her a chart with several peeking lines running across it, none of which she understood. "By all accounts, this is a good sign. Patients in sustained unconscious states don't usually exhibit such vibrant activity."

"That's a good thing then. That means she's going to wake up soon. Doesn't it?"

"Well… we don't know. It usually means they're already awake. As I said, we've never seen anything like this. Mrs. Henderson, it's as if Alex is still going about her life. She's showing the same brain activity as you or I would be showing right now." Barb looked down at her daughter and noticed the rapid eye movements and twitching of her cheeks and lips.

"That's not all," the doctor continued. "You see, I mentioned that when Alex arrived, we had very little injury reported. I did the examination myself, so I know what was there. Only," he hesitated, "There have been some anomalies." He returned his gaze to the clipboard. "At 4:32 pm, about an hour after her arrival, we saw a sudden spike in the electrical levels in her body; the machines had trouble monitoring her and everything connected to her shut down, shorted out." He paused and looked down at his clipboard again.

"Another hour later, we saw another surge of electricity, this one was much more powerful and according to her body movements, the wave seemed to travel across her body and exit the other side. Then of course, you'll remember that today her shoulder dislocated."

"What?" Barb shook her head rapidly from side to side, "What you're saying doesn't make sense. People's shoulders don't just dislocate. One of the staff must have had an accident."

"We know." He put his hand up, an arbitrary motion to try and calm her. "We are doing everything in our power to find out what's going on with your daughter. We will give her as much attention as we can. Obviously, we want to get to the bottom of this as much as you."

Barb highly doubted that, but she was slightly comforted by the urgency in the doctor's voice.

"For now," he continued, "You should get some sleep. We will call you if your daughter's condition changes."

Barb didn't want to leave her daughter's side ever again, but she reluctantly packed her things and headed for home.

# DREAMING

When Alex finally regained consciousness, she found herself in complete darkness. The surface under her was hard, and as she patted through the blackness, the walls, and ground surrounding her seemed cold and metallic. Sitting upright, she recalled the events that had directly preceded her unconscious state. Her shoulder still throbbed.

"Hello?" she called softly, wondering if the other strange shrunken companions were still present, or if they had, in fact, been figments of her imagination. The air filled with sounds of shuffling and quiet murmurs alerting her that wherever she was, she was not alone.

"Careful," a woman's voice came from behind her as two small hands gently helped her sit upright.

"The light, Tilly." The voice Alex recognized as the young woman in the leather jacket came from somewhere in front of her.

"Aaaaaaaw, but the battery is almost dead! If I turn it on, it might be the last time." There was a sound of skin lightly smacking skin and then a low whine. A faint light illuminated the immediate area. It shone from the wrist of one of the other six people that surrounded her. The girl was approximately eight years old, and her red pig tails shot out sideways from her head. Her short, plump body shifted from one foot to the next as she scowled at the floor. The light coming from the wrist device revealed that the instrument was almost too small for the pudgy arm that held it. Alex stared at it with curiosity. The device was about ten centimeters wide with a screen that took up most of its surface. It appeared to be a cruder version of the one she had seen on Ciara's wrist. A faint glow from the screen revealed a grid pattern that lay across the screen. *Why would anyone put a grid on their screen? How are you supposed to see the picture?* Her musings were cut short.

"It's called a PCD, Personal Communications Device." The girl giggled, noticing that Alex was staring. "I'm not supposed to have one. But I found it, and it's mine!" What started as a giggle, turned into the sounds of a whiney toddler.

"Some people have made them do other things, there are loads of mods for them." The girl beside her cut her off, turning on her. "Besides, mom said you have to share if you're going to keep it!" They wore matching knee length red skirts, which flowed around their legs, and yellow button up shirts. Their collars were adorned with large, blue, overbearing bows. Each had a blue ribbon in their hair, but the newest girl, Alex presumed to be Tully, had her hair pulled back into a more severe bun. Both girls filled their shirts to bursting. Every time one of them opened her mouth to speak, the other would counter with a louder argument. Whether the arguments had merit or not Alex couldn't tell because they refused to let each other speak longer than a few seconds.

Turning her attention to the rest of the party, she could see that the others in the compartment were relatively unremarkable. They looked like peasants from medieval England, except their crude clothing while tattered, dirty, and dull, seemed too synthetic for an ancient era. Alex looked around for the young girl who had rushed to her aid earlier and noticed she wasn't in the immediate circle. After a few seconds of searching, she spotted the leather jacket and striped bob peering from a shadowy unlit corner of the room. The girl squatted, her hands on her knees. She looked ready to pounce. The girl crouched motionless as Alex examined her; unblinking and barely breathing. A second later she jerked her head to the side and slunk into a standing position, causing Alex to jump. As she stepped forward out of the shadows, the girl stroked her hair backward with the side of her hand and tucked it behind her ear.

Assuming the girl was the leader of this band of misfit captives, Alex directed her question in her direction. "Who are you? Where am I?"

"Your reactions and questions are predictable, and as usual not the correct ones. Newcomers are always a bit… confused, but soon you will come to know everything you need." *As if this day wasn't puzzling enough!*

"Fine," she retorted, a bit shorter than she would have liked. "What do I call you?"

"You can call me Ches," a smile spread across the girl's face, once again wider than Alex thought humanly possible. Ches tilted her head and stretched before melting into a sitting position.

"Is this a dream?" Alex figured the direct approach was worth a try.

"Many truths that we cling to depend on our point of view. Does it feel like a dream?" Ches tucked the other side of her hair behind her ear, once again using the side of her hand.

"Well," Alex hesitated, "If it's not a dream, then I'm going crazy."

"Perhaps you're not crazy." Ches paused, tapping her finger on her chin and staring off in contemplation. "Have you thought that your reality is just… different than everyone else's?"

In fact, Alex had thought of her life as a dream for some time, or she had hoped it was a dream. For the past eighteen months, she kept thinking that if she woke up, her father would be alive, her mother would be spending more time at home again, and she would return to being an invisible face in the crowded hallways of her school. Perhaps she had woken up, and this was her reality. She couldn't recall feeling pain in her dreams before and judging from the pounding that still lingered in her shoulder, she could definitely feel pain in this… reality.

"Alright, well if this isn't a dream, then what next? What am I supposed to do? How do I get out of this?" Alex clenched her teeth together, stopping herself from lashing out. After all, Ches and the rest of the surrounding party appeared to be captives as well.

"Where do you want to go?" Ches adjusted her position. Her movements were as slow as honey pouring from a bottle. She lay on her back, crossed one leg over the other and placed her hands behind her head. Once again she stretched, arching her back slightly before her entire body went limp.

"I… I don't know…"

"Well then," Ches' smile grew wider. "If you don't know where you need to go, then it doesn't really matter which path you take."

It wasn't the answer she had hoped for, but Ches had closed her eyes and was already starting to doze. Alex looked around at the others in the group, and they all sat quietly offering little in the way of insight. The two pudgy sisters continued to poke and prod each other with bickering whispers, apparently arguing about whether it was time to turn the light off. In a few minutes, the world went dark again, and Alex was left with nothing but her thoughts.

For months, she had been begging someone, anyone, to pluck her out of her current existence and give her something better. Still, the thought of being transported to another reality, for seemingly no good reason at all, was too much for her to believe. If she was honest with herself, she wasn't sure that this reality was any better.

As she pondered, she listened to the hushed voices of the two girls hissing back and forth as they crossed to the other side of the shared prison. The others returned to their respective waiting spots, and Alex realized how tired she was. Her entire body felt heavy under her weight, and she grunted as she lowered herself back down to the ground. As much as she had wished for a new reality, this wasn't what she had in mind. As she drifted off to sleep, she wondered what time it was, or what day it was for that matter. Reaching down, she felt the solid flat phone tucked into her jeans. She wanted desperately to see if it still worked in this world, to check the time, browse her socials, or scroll some videos. She had been used to these distractions, and the lack of comfort from them was like a gaping vacuum in this new reality. It would be distracting to pull it out now, however, and she wasn't sure she wanted to share it with the rest of them. It too would be as dead as the PCD if she had to use it to supply light. Closing her eyes, she wished that it would all be over when she woke, or that at least she would get some answers. As she let herself drift, a click and swish from the compartment door halted her rest.

# PLANS

A bright light invaded the compartment.

"Come, my pets, you're terribly boring today." The high-pitched, cheerful voice that had lured her into the carriage was now low and booming. Alex rubbed her eyes as the light burned her corneas. She was still stuck inside a glove box, but when she had closed her eyes earlier, she hadn't really expected things to change. This world felt too real, and quite honestly, she hadn't really been looking forward to another day of torment and hostility back at school. Even as a captive, she was beginning to think Wonderland was much more exciting than her real life. Then, she wasn't sure that her old life was her real life anymore. Her new companions had referred to her as a newcomer, but what did that mean? As the light woke the others in the cage, she figured she might as well make the best of it. Ches' words rang out in her head. "It doesn't matter where you go then." She didn't know anything about Wonderland, or why was she here, so it didn't really matter where she went? Although, as she looked around her, she was reminded that she didn't really have the option to go anywhere.

The compartment door had opened, and Alex looked over to see a giant eyeball, outlined in thick eyeliner, staring into their shared space. The twins and the other three captives formed a line, awkwardly performing summersaults, dancing, and singing. There was no cohesiveness to their act as they unilaterally entertained. Ches sat in the corner, observing the others and defiantly refusing to join their five-ring circus. This didn't appear to bother Ciara, who apparently had enough to entertain her for now. She shivered to think what might have happened if the show hadn't started on demand. However, Alex also had no intent on staying locked away to find out. She didn't understand why the others didn't just run for it. The compartment was open. They could easily escape before their enormous captor could catch them all. In fact, if they all ran at the same time, it would make it much harder. Maybe they were all too afraid to try, or no one wanted to lead the charge. Still, Alex thought that with Ciara distracted she just might have a chance of jumping free without their jailer noticing. If the others were happy with their captivity, she would leave them to their own devices.

Standing, she sauntered over to the edge of the room, partially doing a jig on the way in case it was a requirement of moving when Ciara was watching them. She made her movements small enough to not draw attention to herself. Inching her way forward, she rocked back and forth on her legs, working up the nerve to jump. She wasn't sure how far the compartment was off the cushion, but she was sure it was much higher for her when she was only a few inches tall. She also had no idea how soft her landing might be. With one final inhalation of breath, she plunged forward.

The neck of her shirt strangled her, as her body became a near projectile. Something, or rather someone, had grabbed her from behind, stopping her escape. She let out a choked grunt as she fell backward on her rump.

"Hey!" she sputtered, rubbing her throat. Their watching captor let out an excited chuckle.

"Oh, I was so hoping you'd let her jump," the voice boomed. In an instant, they were surrounded once again by blackness. Whispered bickering filled the air again and the light around Tilly's pudgy wrist filled the area. Without a word, Ches took a small stone out of her pocket and threw it toward the compartment door. It stopped just short and a red sheet of light lit the front of the chamber. A few tendrils of electricity sprang from the surface of the wall.

Realizing her mistake, Alex let out a hoarse word of thanks and rubbed her neck. At least their continuous captivity made sense now, but she had watched enough movies to know that there was always a way out, she just had to find it. Mumbling quietly, Alex rose to her feet and began to pace. Perhaps they could trick their captor into lowering the shield? Maybe there was a way they could disable it from the inside? Maybe it only hurt while you went through the wall, surely she could stand a few seconds of pain. If only she could see. The light from the PCD was growing dimmer by the second. The battery was obviously depleting, and it wouldn't be long before they were once again in darkness, and they would be unable to do anything but wait. Alex almost offered her phone as a new source, but thought better of it, she didn't know if she'd need it once she got out of this mess and wasn't willing to divulge her secret just yet.

"I told you she'd try and get us out." The whispered bickering from the twins was becoming more audible the longer Alex paced.

"She can't get us out, she just got here. She didn't even know about the wall."

"She's smart, I can tell by looking at her. She's not like the others that have come to Wonderland."

"How do you know that? She hasn't said more than a few words, and everything she's done has been wrong."

"I didn't say she's done smart things. I said she *looks* smart."

The debate grew louder as she tried to think.

"The light is going out soon. She won't be able to see anything. Then what?"

"That's it!" Alex exclaimed. Alex took off her shoe and walked over to the front of the compartment where the ominous hidden wall lay in wait. She carefully placed the runner on the ground and made sure the rubber was touching the floor. As she paced, she had noticed that the edge of the compartment was made of stone instead of metal. Likely, to protect the prisoners from feeling any residual shocks from the electric field that kept them contained.

"What are you doing?" It was one of the female captives. She wasn't old but her plaited brown hair was greying at the temples. Her face turned red to match the ribbon that tied off her braid as she continued. "You're crazy! You're going to kill yourself. You're going to kill all of us." By the time she finished she was in hysterics but one look from Ches, and she slunk back, quieting her protests. Ches continued to watch curiously.

"Turn off your light. Save the battery." Alex turned to the twins.

"But… it's almost dead anyway miss."

"Turn it off!" Her assertiveness was new, and she liked the way it made her feel. She went ahead cautiously, nudging the shoe slowly toward the field. A heat filled bolt sent her stumbling backward as soon as the shoe made contact. It certainly didn't hurt as much as her shoulder had the day before, but she squeaked as it made contact.

The entire compartment was lit with blue waves of light and energy. Tiny bolts of lightning struck out from the field at the shoe. It blackened and smoked, but as she observed her desired effect, Alex smiled. The only unknown was how much energy the field's battery held. If it was hooked to the carriage's main energy supply, then there really was no hope. However, Alex had a hunch that the compartment was a Ciara customization. Surely everyone in Wonderland didn't wander around collecting little people as pets.

The same unconcerned smile sat on Ches's face while the others stood, inching closer in awe with mouths agape at the small grounding object that Alex had made.

"I told you she looks smart," Tully piped up, and Tilly had no retort this time. It didn't take long for the field's light to become so intense that they had to avert their eyes. The shoe was growing more charred with each second, and the rubber sole had already melted to the stone floor. After about a minute, the light from the field began to grow dim. A smile of pride spread across Alex's face. Her father would have been proud of her resourcefulness. When he was alive, he had always joked with her that she was trying to steal his job when she would do something of particular cunning.

Smoke filled the air, and she had a hunch that the compartment wasn't airtight with its own life support system. That meant that it wouldn't be long before Ciara was alerted to their activities and would check on them.

"Get ready to jump!" Alex whispered loud enough for everyone to hear. The woman with the red ribbon began to cry.

"I can't. I...I can't." She shook her head furiously, but her words were barely a squeak.

"*Can't* merely means you haven't yet tried," Ches spoke from a few meters to the right of Alex where she was leaning against the wall. It didn't sound stern. In fact, she almost seemed amused at the situation. *Why on earth did she always have a dramatic and crazy smile on her face!?* Alex wondered. The twins began to bicker about who would jump first.

As expected, seconds after the sparks dissipated, the

compartment slid open and the light burst in, temporarily blinding them. Alex took a deep breath and ran. Without hesitation, she jumped over the edge to the cushion waiting below. She held her breath through her flight, hoping that her captor would be taken by surprise, and fail to react. The other part of her hoped that the cushion was as soft to land on, as it had been to sit on. She landed with minimal impact. The cushion moved her body like a gigantic trampoline, and four muffled thuds sounded behind her. Alex waited for the last two landings but heard nothing. Whipping her head around, and looking up at the compartment ledge, she saw the woman with the red ribbon still on the ledge, crying into a man's shoulder. Alex assumed this must be her husband, and he tightened his arm around her; kissing the top of her head and rubbed her shoulder. His face was awash with regret and defeat, and he shrugged at them.

"Go," he mouthed to them, and they stepped back from the ledge so they were no longer in sight. After the initial shock of flying tiny humans, Ciara was beginning to realize what had happened, and she was furious. She slapped her hand down, grabbing at them, trying to collect them and put them back into her cage. The angry man from earlier was the first to be recaptured. Ciara lifted him and screamed directly at him as he dangled in front of her face.

"Quick!" Alex called to her companions, "Run!" They ran to the edge of the seat cushion and began to climb down as fast as they could to the floor and the small crack under the carriage door. The scene outside whizzed by so fast that it was impossible to see where they were. Their only choice was to jump or be caught, and none of them seemed to want to find out what Ciara would do to them now. Seeing the hesitation on the twins' faces, she knew she had to set the example. Ches nodded at her once, the same smile plastered across her face. Closing her eyes tightly, Alex was soon flying. Once she was out of the carriage, everything slowed to a snail's crawl. She was hurtling through the air toward a fortunately placed pile of discarded food, and she hoped that apple peels and bread were as soft to land on, as they were to chew. She braced for impact, turning her body to avoid landing on her already injured shoulder. An instant later, she bounced off a loaf end and skidded across the cobbles.

# OUT OF THE FRYING PAN...

The twins landed with a thump a few feet ahead of her, thankfully on a pile of grass that had grown out between the cobbles. Ches flipped through the air and landed another small distance ahead of them, her feet firmly planted, with one hand on the ground between her legs. The focused look she wore disappeared and was once again replaced by her wide grin.

Alex rose to her feet, dusting off the crumbs and muck that had clung to her outfit as she rolled through the refuse. Looking around she could see they were clearly now in a city of some sort. A hand pushed her out of the way of the mammoth wooden wheel of a cart traveling past. She nodded her thanks to Tully, whose tight bun had become unraveled leaving her curly red locks to dangle around her shoulders. Hundreds of giants walked along the street, and Alex tried to decide how long it would take for her tiny legs to walk the length of it. Her contemplation ended with a heavy sigh. The entire district was covered in muck and refuse. A stone wall mixed with digital signage rose high above the buildings, broadcasting grim warnings and images creating an ominous ambiance. The current warning read, "All trespassers will be punished!" Someone had gone to a lot of trouble to ensure that no one could see, interfere, or take part in whatever lay on the other side of the wall.

Extending out of the wall, several tubes deposited disc-shaped blocks of metal and plastic that reminded Alex of hockey pucks. No one tried to move them or stack them, and the pile continued to overflow and fill the area. The buildings were made of stone and were reminiscent of a medieval city. The architecture, however, is where the comparison stopped. Doors whooshed open automatically as people passed through them, and windows were free of glass. A blue hue like the one in the compartment could be seen buzzing back and forth across their openings. In front of the buildings stood several carts filled with garments, food, and household goods, which could be bought or traded. For the most part, the people in the city were dressed in clean and dry clothing. Nothing was as fancy and frilly as Ciara's outfit had been, but some bore electrical lights or PCDs that peaked out from their hiding places under sleeves. Some carried money, but most held out their palm as a flat scanner was swept over them completing transactions.

Alex didn't know whether to go off on her own or stay with her newly escaped counterparts. Ches sidled up to her and extended a hand.

"Here," she handed Alex a small square pastry. The cake was white, but the glaze on top morphed from purple to blue to pink and back again. "Eat this."

"Oh," she stuttered, "thank you but I'm not hungry." In fact, Alex was starving, but there was something about a multi-colored flickering food that turned her stomach. The smell of rotting garbage didn't help either.

"Suit yourself," Ches smiled and dropped the square into Alex's hand. She closed her lips around an identical one from a pouch at her side. In a matter of seconds, Alex's tiny new companion was large enough to step on her. The twins didn't hesitate with their tiny morsels either, and their large baby doll shoes were soon placed squarely beside Alex. Hesitating, she placed the morsel between her teeth. A sweet burst of flavour spread over her tongue. At first, it was blackberry then a wash of chocolate followed by raspberry, and a few seconds later pineapple filled her mouth. It was the most intoxicating thing that she had ever eaten. Looking down at her hands and feet, she watched as the large stones beneath them became smaller, or rather her foot became larger, in comparison. No one on the street seemed to pay any attention, as if growing and shrinking people were the norm in this world. While her body returned to its normal size, Ches sauntered over to the side of the road toward a narrow alley between two buildings. The space was barely big enough for her to fit through, but by the time Alex had returned to her regular size, Ches was nowhere to be seen. It was as if she had vanished into thin air.

Alex was left in the middle of the street with Tilly and Tully, who were already bickering. As soon as they noticed Alex looking at them, they fell silent.

"You must come home with us! You must be hungry. Mama and Papa won't mind at all." Their voices were in complete synchronicity. Alex had no desire to follow the two girls home, especially if Ches was gone, and she was desperately looking around for some excuse to part ways.

"I really should be going." She started down the street, randomly picking a direction.

"Nooooo! You can't leave." The whining was more annoying in unison. "You haven't even introduced yourself. Manners, manners, we must remember our manners." They moved as if they were connected by an invisible cord, and blocked Alex from continuing. Their skirts and bows swayed back and forth with the movement.

"I'm Alex." She stepped backward, hoping to make a clean break in the other direction.

"Alex," they spoke with one voice. "Such a lovely name. You must have tea, Alex, perhaps a game of Bikerat."

Taking another step backward, Alex tried for distraction. Even though she had already discerned their names, she opted for polite conversation. "Speaking of manners, you haven't given me your names either."

"I'm Tilly," said the one who still wore her PCD.

"I'm Tully," the other sister chimed in as if the entire response was one sentence. In fact, if Alex had closed her eyes, she would not have been able to tell them apart. She looked around for some mode of escape or at least some distraction that would allow her to go off on her own. What she needed was a quiet space to figure things out.

The girls began bickering again, about who would ask their mother and father if Alex could stay for tea, and Alex took the opportunity to scan the street. Out of the corner of her eye, she noticed a most peculiar thing. A tall human-shaped robot walked along the street. It stood out in stark contrast to the rest of its surroundings. Its body was made of a pure white metallic material, and transparent plastic windows on its chest, biceps, calves, and quads allowed a full view of the solid gold cogs underneath.

The device didn't move like other robots she had seen. Instead, it had all the fluid movements of a human without the squishy exterior. She stared at the device… robot… android… man… as it zig-zagged its way through the crowds of people. It was preoccupied and didn't notice its audience of one. Hardly anyone paid attention to it, and those that did looked on with scorn.

"Oh dear, oh dear, I'm late again." Its voice was distinctly male with a slight synthetic buzz. He moved along checking a small pocket-watch every few seconds. Each time he opened it a floating holographic clock face appeared hovering a few centimeters above the watch's surface. Alex moved to follow, trying to push past the girls, but they refused to budge. Their tiny plump bodies were much more solid than Alex had expected.

"It looks like she's a curious one," Tilly said to Tully.

"I hope no one finds out," Tully gasped. "You know what happened to the last one."

"I'm sure it wouldn't happen again. At least, I'd hate for it to happen again," Tilly responded.

"Oh, how dreadful that would be. You don't think… No, I'm sure she wouldn't do it again."

"What?" Alex stopped abruptly, focusing her attention back on the girls, "You hope what doesn't happen again?" Knowing they had succeeded in grabbing her attention, they parted and walked around either side of Alex until they were behind her.

"We dare not speak of it," said Tully.

"Besides, I'm sure it would never happen again," said Tilly.

"You're in a terrible hurry anyway, I'm sure you don't have time to hear the tale." This last statement was once again in unison. The twins casually began to walk away. Devious smirks spread across their faces.

"No, wait," Alex called after them. "I have time. Tell me what happened." She was completely drawn in by their trap, swiveling and following them as they walked down the street. They walked past shops, weaved up and down alleyways, and finally climbed onto a cart, pausing for dramatic effect as they spun their tale.

# CURIOSITY

"Every day she walked the streets, back and forth with carts of beets, but never did she seem to stay, upon the path endorsed that day." Tilly and Tully began their tale in harmony, a look of triumph on their faces as they lured Alex through the streets with their words.

"The world's so big, and much too bright, to stay the course each day and night," Tully added the first part of the story, and the girls continued alternating one line after the next.

"Her Ma would scold, and Pa would warn, of dangers lurking beyond the corn."

"Farming life was much too bleak, and she longed for just a peek."

"At the world outside the farm, without her folk raising alarm."

"Then one dark night, without a sound, she set out and a city found."

"It buzzed and whirred like nothing she'd seen and was like no place she'd ever been."

"The people looked a lot like her until she followed the dark one's lure."

"With lights and sounds it moved along, she naturally followed its mechanical song."

"Legend says she never came back, once past the gate beyond the shack. For without the Queen's royal okay, behind the wall, we all must stay."

"Evil waits to scrape and chafe but do what's right and you'll be safe."

The whole story sounded like a childhood song meant to warn or scare them away from something their parents didn't want them to see. It was clearly a form of propaganda intended to control the children in this world. Alex wondered how the girls could have ever been captured if they were so scared of going off the usual path. The mesmerizing little tune had brought them to the edge of the city though it had seemed to last a few moments. The houses were growing sparser, and the land was dotted with periodic fields. Alex noticed that the wall that had been prominent along the street in the city was nowhere to be seen. Confusion rose as she wondered at the haste of their travel. Looking back, she noticed that the city was, in fact, a lot larger than she had thought. From this vantage point, it appeared to be built in a circular pattern. Around the outside of the city, piles of refuse surrounded a dark, dirty looking muddle of buildings piled one on top of the other. The lower portion of the city was by far the largest, and it sprawled across the landscape like a spreading puddle of ooze. The entire city rose up in the middle on a hill. At its pinnacle lay an elegant stone castle. A few typical towers rose up to brush the sky, but at least twelve newly erected towers contrasted with the old architectural design. The towers were a flat rectangle, twisted upward, and ending in a teardrop shaped point. The walls of these new towers were reflective, casting light upon the buildings below. A myriad of large buildings, in-filled with trees, stood proudly around the area. In a similar fashion to the castle, each building had a new tower that spiraled upward like twisted skyscrapers. Clear tubes attached some of the towers, and every so often she could see objects hovering through the air, though she was too far away to make them out.

It was absolutely beautiful. The shining buildings and lush gardens that surrounded them mesmerized Alex. Of course, surrounding the beautiful cityscape, as if to protect it from the filthy city that lay beyond, was the great cocooning wall. It rose as high as most of the buildings beyond it, and Alex could clearly see there were several entrances stationed around the perimeter. At the bottom of the circle, the walls continued in a straight line outward, following a cobbled road. It created a perfect trench-like access to the most extravagant part of the city.

The spot in the wall she assumed she had come from seemed kilometers away. She had been so wrapped up in the tale the twins had recited that she hadn't noticed the distance they had come. In unison, the twins once again began to speak. "Every day she walked the streets, back and forth with carts of beets, but never did she seem to stay, upon the path endorsed that day." The rhythmic chant was hypnotic, and Alex began to fall back into step with the girls. Realizing their pull, she shook her head back to awareness. As she thought back over the past forty-five minutes to an hour, she remembered hearing the same story several times. Each time the story started she had looked around, wondering where she was and how she had gotten there, and each time she fell back into step and followed the girls even further out of the city. Like lightning, her hands traveled to her ears, blocking out the chant. She stopped and stared at the girls, who suddenly seemed to realize that she was aware of their scheme. The realization sent them into a flinching tremor. Their words repeated as their heads twitched. For the first time, Alex noticed their semi-robotic movements.

"Every d...d...day..."

"Every day she wa... wa...lked" They shivered, tremors traveling from their pigtails to their perfectly shined shoes and glanced at each other. In one fluid movement, their hands clamped together, and their child-like appearance faded away. Millions of tiny insect-like particles moved across the surface of their skin and the girls melted into each other, forming one solid black mass before shifting into a large ink-black creature. Whatever it was, it appeared to be encased in a solid black suit of armor. Its head and face were completely covered, leaving only a small thin opening at eye level. Its joints and limbs were seamless as the particles continued to flow fluidly across the surface of its new body. On its chest, a glowing red spade formed as an indentation like a brand, and its eyes glowed with matching luminosity. Alex began to back away from the ominous shape, slowly and desperately trying to not attract its attention as she plotted her escape.

"Newcomers must be captured and disposed of, by order of the Queen." The robotic directive was matched with an equally mechanical voice. The massive black humanoid mass lifted its right arm, and a small door opened in its forearm. Out of it rose a long metal tube topped with a glass vial filled with a glowing green liquid. Alex ducked as she heard the click and pressed her body into the muddy ground. The dart that projected out of the weapon whipped by, narrowly missing her ear and with a twang, stuck into the side of a nearby house. Immediately, the house began to dematerialize in a similar fashion as the monster in front of her had materialized, beginning at the spot where the dart hit. Alex watched as the interior of the house came into view, its crude furnishings exposed to the elements. Seemingly unaware at first what was happening, a woman inside stood in the center of the kitchen. A large computerized machine on the counter looked out of place when compared with the rest of the fixtures. She pressed a few buttons and several ingredients poured out of tubes in the top of the machine, landing in a large mixing bowl. Judging by the smell that wafted out of the house, she was preparing the evening meal. As the walls deteriorated further, she looked around wildly and shrieked. Desperately, she tried to pull a large canvas sheet over the contraption, and seemed relieved when the black mass paid her no mind.

Alex jumped to her feet and bolted, running between the buildings, ducking under wagons and toppling any obstacle she could move. Every time she thought she had put an impassable obstacle between them, her pursuer would liquefy, and the black ooze would make its way around or under the blockade before rematerializing on the other side. It never ran, but never waivered in its methodical pursuit. Its pace afforded Alex some extra time while ducking and jumping, but somehow the machine always found her. It was ironic, because if she had been asked to do this in gym class, she would have sighed and rolled her eyes. Faced with death, the actions came naturally, as if she had been doing them for years. It was clear. If she were going to rid herself of her pursuer, she would have to do something more than run.

Ahead she noticed a large murky pool surrounded by more piles of refuse. Back at home, electronics and water were never a good combination, and she felt it was her only hope. Various pipes emptied into the pond from all sides, it unclear where they had come from and what exactly was draining into the pond. Without a second thought, she plugged her nose and plunged into the murky water. The pond was, at least, thirty meters across and as she waded, she could feel the viscous liquid resisting her retreat. She splashed out until she was chest deep in the putrid smelling liquid and turned around to await her fate. The creature stopped and looked down, hesitating before proceeding into the pool. Alex cursed and whirled around splashing as she paddled toward the other side of the pond, trying hard not to splash her face. Her feet sank into the muck with each step. After a few moments, however, the machine started to slow. The particles that had been able to morph into any shape they wanted moments ago became a gyrating mass of material, unable to assume any form at all. After a few minutes of struggle, the spinning blob dropped into the pool, its inky black hue spreading across the surface of the water like a slick of oil. It no longer seemed to have any directional purpose.

"It usually takes people ages to figure out how to evade the guards." An amused male voice came from behind her. She whirled around to see a tall young man, slightly older than her, standing on the bank, leaning against one of the wagons nearby. "Of course, I probably wouldn't have chosen to take a swim in the sewer if it had been me."

# FRIEND OF FOE

*Was everyone in this world so rude?!* she thought. The thick soupy liquid sloshed as she moved toward the edge of the pond, glaring at her new companion. She wrinkled her nose, trying to keep from expelling any of the food remaining in her stomach.

The young man's garments were plain, and he was relatively unremarkable when compared to the farmers that worked in their yards around the area. He held out his hand as she came closer to the shore. Grateful for the help, she grasped his calloused hand and pulled herself up and out of the gunge. Thick brown sludge stained her clothes, dripping from her outstretched limbs. She immediately felt for her phone and pulled it out of her pocket. Trying the button, she was met with a powerless void. She cursed and focused her attention back to the dripping apparel that imprisoned her body.

"Here, let me get that for you." Holding out his hand, he pointed his fist at her before pressing a button on his own wrist device. She ducked, remembering what happened the last time she trusted someone with one of those things. He reached out and caught her before she toppled back into the pool of waste. A bright yellow light poured out of the device. Starting at her head, he moved the beam slowly down her body. As the light moved across her skin, hair, and clothing, the refuse disappeared, leaving her completely spotless and dry. The beam was cozy and it felt like a giant hair dryer was pointed at her. She allowed the beam to move across her, welcoming its gentle warmth. It was the most pleasant thing she had felt since arriving in Wonderland.

"I'm Thomas," he offered, lowering his arm. With the absence of wet, cold sewage dripping from her, she was able to appreciate the young man's features more than her first impressions had allowed. His tanned skin complimented the dark hair that lay tussled around his cheeks. He appeared to be a little older than Alex, as he had a small showing of whiskers peaking through in well-tended patches on his face. His eyes, however, were the most striking, reminding Alex of silvery blue event horizons in a Stargate.

"Alex," she responded, sighing a little with disappointment as the warmth disappeared, making the air around her seem extra cool. A growl rose from her stomach as she slipped the now useless phone back into her pocket, reminding her that she hadn't eaten anything substantial since arriving.

"Hungry, are we?" Thomas chuckled. "Let me take care of that." He motioned with his head for her to follow and walked toward a nearby house. Ches' words popped into her head. *"If you don't know where you need to go, then it doesn't really matter which path you take."* She figured that it was good enough advice, and, at least, he didn't seem like an enemy. However, she hadn't thought the twins would turn on her either.

The houses in this area were further apart than those she had seen from her shrunken state. However, since she had escaped Tilly and Tully's cyborg trap, she could no longer see the city skyline. She had made her way back toward the interior of the city when she fled, and the buildings around them were now denser, blocking her view of the castle, and the stunning district beyond the wall. The area was less developed than the market she had found herself in before, but the residents here were clearly more than simple farmers. The occasional shop peppered the area, but most of the district seemed to be made up of one story residences.

She followed the young man as he entered a small single story house made of wooden planks. The cracks were filled with mud and straw, and the roof was covered with clay shingles. Unlike the buildings deeper in the city, there was nothing remarkable about the home. The windows bore real glass, and a small garden grew out front. A fenced area, holding a few goats, was nestled next to the thriving plants.

The barren house had a main room with two doors to assumed bedrooms. A tidy kitchen, a small living space, and a solid wood table that served multiple purposes. Parchment, books, and dishes were scattered on it. A hearth and chairs were on the left wall, while a cooking area with a wood stove was on the right. Despite signs of life, no one was there. When asked, the young man avoided the question and locked the door. He moved to a switch, and Alex braced herself for impact. Instead, the house transformed. The fireplace was replaced with a sleek tube from floor to ceiling. A multi-coloured fire burned at its base, and heat was pushed out through holes about halfway up. The tube wasn't made of a material. Instead, the fire was protected by an energy field, similar to the windows in the other part of the city. The top of the table, seemingly solid wood moments ago, opened to reveal a large screen, which took up most of its real estate. She watched intently as the last of the wooden cover disappeared into the side of the table leaving only a small frame along the edge wide enough for a cup or bowl. The kitchen seemed to have undergone the largest transformation. Most of the renovation had happened before she opened her eyes, but she watched as a final metal box rose out of the floor, completing the ensemble of matching appliances. There didn't appear to be any burners or cooking surfaces, which Alex thought odd. The main focus in the new kitchen, however, was a solid slab of black stone material. A single cylinder was mounted on the cabinet above it, and a few lights flickered as it sprang to life. Out of the ceiling dropped a multi-tiered planter with various fruits, vegetables, and herbs sprouting from it at every angle.

"Replicator food is great, but it lacks that bit of freshness that one craves from time to time." Thomas smirked at her wide-eyed surprise.

Walking forward slowly, she let her eyes graze upon the new interior. "Where did it all come from?"

"Strictly speaking, we aren't supposed to have tech in The Cistern."

Remembering her swim from earlier she wrinkled her nose. "The Cistern?"

"It's what she calls this district. Most of the locals hate the name too, but you know how it is."

"Actually, I don't."

"Oh... right... new girl."

"Everyone keeps saying that, like I have a tattoo across my forehead." Her hand went to her forehead. It wouldn't be that unusual considering everything she had been through already today. Taking a seat at the table she reached instinctively for the phone in her back pocket. Remembering its lifeless state, she placed it on the table with a clunk and it slid across the surface, stopping just before it teetered off the edge.

Thomas chuckled, "There's no tattoo. It's just, most people are used to things around here. You can tell when someone new arrives by the sheer wonder, or horror, on their faces... and their new gadgets."

"Are there a lot of...*new* people around here?" She scanned the room as the buzzing and whooshing stopped. It looked nothing like it had previously. Some of the furniture was similar in outward appearance, but instead, there were screens, lights, and chrome-covered boxes everywhere.

"We haven't seen anyone new for," he counted on his fingers, "well not since I've been alive. I've only heard the stories."

"How... did I get here?" As she moved to the kitchen table, she noticed an electronic map was being projected from the surface. In the center, she recognized the circular city. Beyond the city, to the South and East, lay a giant forest of trees. A sea bordered the West with a few          smaller villages dotting the coastline, and to the North, mountains blocked a desert area beyond. Directly East of the city, the map was grayed out. Before Alex could examine the map further, the image began to morph. It zoomed in, and soon the entire table was covered with a rotating maze of streets.

The Cistern, as Thomas had called it, stretched for kilometers around the inner district. Even on the map, the Cistern looked decrepit and abused. Most of the houses stood out in vivid detail, and Alex couldn't resist playing with it any longer. Making her way to the table, she tapped her finger on one of the houses and the map stopped rotating. Slowly, the house grew on the screen, as an unseen eye zoomed in on the surrounding area. Once the image was static, Alex prodded the screen again, and the image grew to take up the entire screen. In the dirt yard, two children chased a glowing, floating orb around. Even though Alex couldn't hear them, she could see their laughter as the orb swooped around their heads, stopping to hover close to their necks, making them giggle and shy away. A woman stood nearby hanging clothing and sheets on a line. She cautiously looked around, as if she hoped no one was watching.

When the kids strayed too far away from the yard, Alex could see her mouth moving, yelling for them to come back.

"Is this real?" Alex looked up to see Thomas watching her intensely. He seemed amused by her ignorance, which gave Alex a pang of self-consciousness. Had she not endured enough ridicule for one day? Not waiting for him to answer, she stood abruptly and made for the door.

"Thanks, but I prefer not to hang out with people who just want to laugh at me." Her words were harsh, but she could tell they struck home because Thomas lost his smile.

"You're getting the wrong idea." He put out his arm to bar her from leaving.

"Ohh, so I'm stupid too? Typical." She tried to push past him. It was out of character for her to talk back, but there was something about being shrunk, enlarged, and almost vaporized that made Alex feel that she could do anything.

"It's just, I don't meet many people who are pretty, excited about tech, *and* know how to use it. I was happy, that's all." When Alex stopped struggling to get past, she looked back up and his expression had changed from amusement to apology. In truth, she had stopped struggling at the word pretty, unsure what to do with it. When she abandoned her retreat, he continued.

"It's an optical monitoring output. I've tapped into the feed being broadcast to the city guards. The satellites were launched several years ago, and it's a way for the Queen to keep tabs on us, keep us in our place." He tapped the screen a few times and the whole image once again began to rotate and zoom. Soon a picture of an area similar, if not identical, to the house she was in, appeared on the screen. As she peered closer, she heard a door close. Her head snapped up, and Thomas was no longer present. The table beeped, and Alex returned her gaze to the movement on the screen. She watched as Thomas waved and smiled up at her. After a minute, he made his way to the door and re-entered the house. The feed was instantaneous. Alex remembered her father talking about boosting satellite feeds to allow instantaneous tracking of targets, but that technology was still decades away. Although it wouldn't be the first unbelievably advanced technology she had encountered since her arrival, she couldn't help being a little excited.

Thomas walked over to the counter, and the large black stone surface. "Grilled cheese times two," he said. The sandwiches that appeared were burnt around the edges, but the cheese oozed out of them making Alex once again remember how hungry she was. Before serving them, he pulled a pouch from his side and took out one a few of the many vials it held. He sprinkled a fine green powder over each and brought them to the table.

"I'm still tweaking its settings." He smiled at her as he handed her the plate. As he sat, he pressed a few more points on the screen and the map disappeared, replaced by the image of a clear blue mountain stream running through the table. Unlike the screens, she had seen along the road and around the city, this river was clearly a digital representation. Every few minutes, the same fish would swim from left to right, and it appeared to loop, indicating it wasn't a live feed.

Hesitating, she waited for Thomas to take the first bite. Clearly, he wasn't trying to poison her, because he had almost finished the sandwich two bites later. When she finally partook, the cheese was warm and sharp; her teeth sank into the toasted crust. A wave of comfort spread over her, and she recognized the green powder as thyme. If nothing else, Thomas knew how to cook, even if most of the meal was replicated.

"Where did you get it all," Alex motioned with her head around the room, mumbling as she chewed.

"Mostly scrounged from The Wasteland beyond the city." Seeing her question, he continued. "The Wasteland is where the people in The Park send all the stuff they no longer want, and before you ask, The Park is the district beyond the wall. It's easy enough to get your hands on tech, the harder part is figuring out how to use it, hide it, and power it."

"Clearly, you've figured it out. Why doesn't everyone else just do the same?"

Thomas took their plates and ran them through a beam of light beside the food replicator. They went into one side of the beam and came out the other side completely spotless.

"Organic dematerializer," he answered her unspoken question without missing a beat and placed the plates back on the slab where they faded into its surface before continuing with the answer to her question. "Let's just say I have an aptitude for this kind of thing."

He puffed out his chest a bit as he continued. "I was able to get my hands on some solar cells, I've worked them into the roof as inconspicuously as I can, as to not draw attention. If anyone found out that I had all this, I'd be de-materialized for certain. The Queen and her court think that if we have too much technology, we'll have an advantage over them, and rise up against them." He walked back to the table and sat next to her. "I suppose they're right because I don't know anyone that wouldn't like to see the whole regime fall. Still, you saw what the guards can do if you cross the Queen or disobey the rules. I've even heard some people pine for the old days when the worst that would happen is *off with your head*." He made a cutting motion with his thumb across his neck.

# TALES

Recognizing the phrase Alex perked up. "What do you mean the old days?"

Thomas walked over to the fireplace and took a book off the mantel. It was a leather-bound volume that appeared very old. He placed it on the table and it fell open. The pages were blank and covered with a glowing grid of lines. Alex jumped back slightly as a holographic image sprang from the pages. The image was of a short fat woman in a red dress. Her image was static but three-dimensional as it spun in the air.

"This is the Red Queen. She was the ruler of this land before her death. She wasn't a saint by any means. If you crossed her, she would order her guards to lop off your head. Even with the threat of death, it was easy enough to avoid the castle grounds. For the most part, the people around the city lived in harmony. However, she extended the same love to her sister as she did to most of her subjects, which, of course, infuriated her sister. She had disappeared for several years into the forest, and the Queen didn't even send a search party out. Some say the Queen was happy to be rid of her sister."

"Those are the days people pine for?" Alex interrupted.

"Yes, but it gets worse. Lindzel, the Queen's sister, had aptitudes similar to mine. She had gone away to look for new and exciting things that would give the advantage she desired over her sister. When she returned, she had nothing but the dress on her back." A new image popped up in front of them. She was much taller and thinner than her sister. Her dark hair hung loosely around the tattered shoulders on her dress. The jagged hem of her skirt barely covered her legs. Despite her mournful and pleading face, she was strikingly beautiful with her blue eyes standing out against her alabaster skin.

"It was only a matter of days before the Red Queen became ill. Some say her sister poisoned her, some say it was just poor luck. I tend to think that Lindzel found some technology that gave her the advantage she had gone searching for. There is no way to really know what happened, and the stories that do exist have all morphed into legends and child's tales. The only truth that we know for certain is that a week later a new Queen was crowned." The hovering image changed. Lindzel was still the focus, but her dress had changed. The fresh style matched that of the woman Alex had met in the carriage earlier that day. The skirt was higher in the front, showing off her knees and tall black boots. The main difference was the cascading train that flowed like an inky black pool of oil on the ground behind her. The dress was completely void of color, and the high collar surrounded her entire head, making her look even paler. An opening at her chest shaped like a spade revealed her skeletal chest. Hanging down into the gap was a single jeweled spade that matched her dress' motif. Like Ciara, the hair on Lindzel's head was twisted into a series of chaotic braids and spikes protruding from her head and was held in place by a jeweled band.

"It didn't take long before the Queen commissioned everyone who knew anything about technology in the castle to work for her. At first, it was glorious, and some even thought that a golden age had finally come. New power sources, nanotechnology, virtual worlds, unlimited replicating food sources, and many more feats of ingenuity graced the scene. The people rejoiced at the new Queen, but the more power she obtained, the greedier she became until her heart was as black as her wardrobe. People started to disappear, and most of them never came back. Soon, everyone was scared to admit they had any creative talent."

"I can see you have a lot of... creative talent." Alex was embarrassed at her own attempt to flirt the minute it came out of her mouth. She didn't know what compelled her to think this handsome, and obviously intelligent boy would pay any attention to her. Certainly, none of the boys at school had paid her any mind, ever. She stood and strode across the room, trying to distract

Thomas from noticing her mistake. He didn't react to notice her transgression, or he was too polite to show his disinterest in her.

"With new nano-builders available, it didn't take long until walls were constructed around The Park. At the request of the residents in the more fortunate part of the city, guards were posted, and the rest of us were locked out of the inner city. Now, only those taking supplies into the area are permitted past the guards, and they are sent through a series of rigorous security clearances before being granted access." Alex could suddenly feel him standing directly behind her as she scanned a bookshelf. His body was still far enough away to be respectful, but she could feel the warmth of his breath as he spoke. "More innovations poured from the castle. However, even though many of the people from the lower city were the founders of these discoveries, everyone from the Cistern was banned from obtaining the new gadgets."

Alex whirled around, her eyes staring directly at Thomas' chin. His closeness was getting a bit too uncomfortable for her to bear. It wasn't that she didn't like the smell of him. In fact, he smelled faintly of cloves, and she enjoyed the feeling of someone that wasn't family, or someone pushing her up against a locker, being so close. However, the longer he lingered, the easier it would be for him to see her imperfections. She ran her hand unconsciously up her arm.

"Oh... " She stepped back until her rear side rested on the bookshelf. "Uh... and then what happened?" The question was clunky, and she knew it. Thomas' smile widened at her response, but he seemed to take the cue that he was making her slightly uncomfortable, and he walked back across the room to sit at the table before continuing.

"Of course, with an increase in electronic innovation, came an increased need for power. The chief engineers had an impossible task ahead of them, but they eventually came up with the ultimate power source. Within months, the ring was constructed to the North East of the city. It was amazing and promised to harness an immense amount of power from the sun."

"So far, aside from the segregation, none of this seems that bad? What could be wrong with a renewable energy source? It sounds like we need that back in my world," Alex interrupted. She had cleared her mind of girlish fancy and was once again rapt in the science being presented.

"Let's just say it didn't turn out exactly how everyone intended. The forest around the rings began to twist and decay. The infection spread quickly, but it didn't stop the Queen. Her followers continued to demand more, and she delivered. The power requirements continued to increase, more rings were constructed, and the blight on the land continued to spread. Nothing will grow for kilometers around the rings now."

He closed the book, and the hologram disappeared in a puff of dust. "Newcomers were frequent during those times. The Queen, or rather her slaves, figured out a way to transport them from other worlds. Using their knowledge, she continued to advance her own power and longevity. However, once the land started to die, rumblings began, and the rebellion was born. Most of the newcomers began to side with the people, and it didn't take long for Lindzel to figure out how to stop people from coming to Wonderland."

"What about me? Why am I here, and what am I supposed to do now?"

"First of all, you are hard to miss. We're going to have to work on that."

"But, *how* does she keep them out? Why am I here?"

Thomas shrugged, and Alex's shoulders sank. When she first arrived, she thought it was the answer to her prayers. However, she wasn't too fond of being shrunk, chased, almost vaporized, and being stuck in a city where the nearest swimming hole was a sewage pond.

"Perhaps you could ask Oothro?"

"Uh… Oothro?"

"Well," he hesitated, "I don't know that I should have even brought it up, but you seem desperate. Of course, you could always just try to blend in. Life here isn't that bad once you get used to it. You're resourceful, I'm sure you could find somewhere to work." Alex half smiled in response; unconvinced.

"Let me guess, Oothro is some old hermit in the forest." She almost chuckled at the cliché.

"Um… not exactly." Thomas still hesitated. He studied her for a few more minutes as if contemplating whether or not she could be trusted before continuing. "Yes, Oothro is in the forest, he never stays in the same place for long, but he's never more than a few day's walk. You'll want to approach with an open mind."

"Oooookay, that's not cryptic at all," Alex let out a forced chuckle. "Should I be worried I'm going to be vaporized?" She was half joking, but, at this point, any prospect of leaving the city sounded great. The best thing about it was that she could finally find some solitude. "How do I find this... *Oothro?*"

"Well... You can probably find someone to direct you in the market, but most of them will have gone home for the evening. In the meantime," he walked over to the window and peeked past the shade. Through the thin crack, Alex could see that night had fallen. How long had they been talking? Perhaps the days were shorter here. Although, she wasn't even sure when she had arrived in Wonderland, and being locked in a cage with no windows certainly hadn't given her any sense of time. He walked across the room to one of the closed doors leading off the living area. "You can sleep here."

The door creaked open as if it hadn't been used in years. As Alex approached, she could make out the shape of a large bed. Once the room was in full view, she could see that it was comfortable, even if it was covered in dust. The side table, bed, dresser, and chair looked much like the furniture in the rest of the house. The only stark difference was the complete lack of tech in this room. Clearly Thomas hadn't gotten around to retrofitting this part of the house. Come to think of it, Thomas seemed rather young to be living alone, especially in a futuristic medieval town, where cyborgs hunted you in the streets. Remembering his response the last time she'd asked a question, she decided not to ask. Exhaustion from the day overtook her, and she decided that the conversation was better left until breakfast.

"Thank you," she mumbled and stepped into the room. The door closed softly behind her, and creaking rose from the hall floorboards as Thomas walked away. For about five minutes, she listened to the familiar buzzing and whooshing that had accompanied the deconstruction of the living area. Thomas must have thought it was safer to put things away for the evening. Another door closed softly, and the light under the door disappeared.

The bed was soft, and as Alex took the weight off her feet, she noticed a single framed picture on the side table. Its dark black screen sprang to life as she approached, and a single picture, or perhaps video, glowed to life. It reminded Alex of a GIF. A woman, only slightly older than Thomas, sat with a baby on her lap. A young man that had been out of frame ran in and stood behind the two. He smiled down at them, cooing at the baby before they all posed, directing the baby to look up at the camera. Everything froze, and the picture reset.

Once she had relaxed into unconsciousness, an image of her father lit up the cinema in her head. He was sitting at his worktable, smiling at her, and waving for her to sit and join him. As she approached, she could see that he had a glowing orb on the table in front of him, but it was in pieces, all it's parts laid out neatly. She thought it was peculiar that he would be working on something that she had only learned of today, but then again, that's usually how dreams worked didn't they? She sat beside him, and warmth radiated from him. All she wanted to do was curl up in his arms, but she could hear his voice trying to break through the veil that blocked all sound out of her dream. Instead, an indecipherable string of words left his lips. He appeared to be trying desperately to relay something to her. Instead, periodic static escaped his lips.

"A...ex... you must... a... do...t... " The string of syllables made little sense. His hands rested on her shoulders, and his gaze was intensified. His words seemed important, however, with her lack of comprehension, she simply relaxed into the enjoyment of his touch.

# VANISHED

The sun streamed through the window, casting a warm band across Alex's cheek. She took a deep breath and sighed heavily. It had been an amazing night, the dreams she had would last at least the morning before someone at school would ruin her day. Her hands stretched above her head, and she arched her back as she opened her eyes. Her jeans pinched at her side, and she wondered why she had gone to bed with her clothes on. When she finally opened her eyes, her head jerked back and forth, taking in her unfamiliar surroundings. After a few moments, she recognized it as the room she had fallen asleep in the night before. The frame on the side table brightened at her movement, and the same image of a happy family posing for a picture greeted her. *Of course I'm still here.* Rubbing her temples, she swung her legs over the edge of the bed and made for the kitchen. Morning fog still filled her head as she contemplated her day's journey. There was apparently a crazy old man in the forest that she had to find, who would have all of life's answers. With any luck, once she was out of the city, she could find a way out of this world and back home. While she wasn't happy with her life there, at least it was familiar. Thomas was already awake and busying himself with various screens and devices around the kitchen. He appeared to be studying the table-top screen intently.

"There are some clothes in the bathroom, the door on the far right." He didn't look up.

She decided not to disturb him and headed straight to the bathroom. The clothes were slightly too big, but they seemed to match the style she had seen most often yesterday. Alex assumed they belonged to the woman in the photo. The simple leather boots were soft around her feet, fitting more snugly than the rest of the clothes did, and the brown pants he had laid out were practical. The tunic, however, was far from plain. She had never imagined herself wearing something as soft and delicate, and feminine. Much to her mother's dismay, most of Alex's wardrobe consisted of jeans and t-shirts. The lack of feminine interests meant that she had spent more time with her father, which suited Alex just fine. There were times that Alex hoped for a girl's day, where she would get a complete makeover, especially once Tasha and her gang started noticing her. By the time she was interested, however, her mother had already seemed to have given up and it never happened. Alex was content to tinker in her father's shop, taking apart and putting together anything she could get her hands on, and learning how things worked, whenever she got the opportunity.

The soft blue material made her feel exquisite as it slipped over her head. The light blue, almost green, fabric looked like linen but felt like cashmere. Its neckline came down in a v, and the sides were fitted, although it hung slightly looser on her than she imagined it was supposed to. Up the sides, a line of corseted loops held the fabric together, and each lace was finished with a simple wooden bead, painted with blue and white designs. When she returned to the table, Thomas was putting the books, and other devices he had been working on, away. The map of the city was displayed on the table.

"What are you doing?" She tried to pretend it was only a mild interest, but in reality, she was completely entranced by his work. His answer wasn't what she expected.

"I'm looking for a way in." His response was short and final, and he walked over to the machine to order breakfast.

"In where?" Alex didn't give up. She didn't think that Thomas was trying to be secretive, and her curiosity had always gotten the better of her. *Besides*, she thought, *I'm going to need as much information as possible if I'm going to run off into a strange world by myself.*

"The Park." He set two bowls of oatmeal on the table and began eating. Clearly, if she was going to get any substantial information from him, she was going to have to try a different approach.

"Where are your parents?" She could see that the question struck a chord. Thomas paused with his spoon halfway to his mouth and sighed deeply. After a few seconds, the spoon descended slowly and rested in the bowl.

"They were…. taken." He exhaled heavily.

Alex stared at him silently, patiently waiting for him to continue, and after a few minutes gathering his thoughts, he continued.

"It was my fault. I've always been too curious for my own good. I would spend my free time in the piles, looking for cool tech to bring home. My parents didn't approve of course. They wanted me to grow up, follow the status quo, and be a simple farmer. But, that wasn't enough for me." He shifted uncomfortably in his chair as he recalled the memory. Somehow, his vulnerability made him even more attractive than she had found him the day before. Alex resisted the urge to walk over and place her hand on his. "I would hide what I found, and work on it after they had gone to bed. I was too young to realize the consequences of being seen with the things that I managed to create. The guards are happy to let us keep simple things like the glowing orb we saw the other day. Even basic PCDs that shed light, or tell the time, are allowed. I, however, had found some communicators. I wanted desperately to make them work, and I gave one of the devices to my friend and told him to guard it closely."

Thomas paused in his retelling and walked over to the window. He peered out for several minutes, breathing deeply as if trying to stifle his emotions. This time, Alex gave into her urge and placed her hand on his shoulder in support. She knew what it was like to lose a parent, and she wanted to give him the silent strength she knew he needed. In response, Thomas' shoulders relaxed and the tension that had been building in them seemed to melt away.

"The day we finally got it to work was glorious." He turned to look at her and her hand moved from his shoulder and down his arm until it rested in his hand. She pulled away from him, embarrassed at the touch, but he managed to grab her hand before she could withdraw fully. "We could talk through the night, telling jokes and stories whenever we wanted. For an eight-year-old, it seemed like we had found the holy grail of toys. Unfortunately, Jonas was prone to bouts of bragging, and he began to show it to the other kids in the city. It didn't take long for the guards to find it." Thomas was unsure what happened during the confrontation, but what he was sure of was that the entire family, including Jonas, had been 'vanished'.

"When they traced the last communication, it led them here. My parents weren't willing to risk everything to resist arrest, however, so they were taken. The only reason I wasn't taken was because I hid under my bed. My father had built the cubby under the floorboards when the Black Queen began to turn for the worse." He paused; his breath short as he looked off into the distance for a few seconds.

"The sound of my mother's agonizing screams pierced through the walls as a group of menacing figures dragged her out of our home. Despite my father's eerie silence, his intense gaze through the cracks in the floor sent shivers down my spine as they ransacked my room in search of something." A single tear rolled down his face, and this time Thomas appeared to be the embarrassed one because he drew away and hid his face as he moved back toward the kitchen, his hands rubbing his eyes casually as he walked. The connection Alex felt with Thomas was greater at that moment than anyone else she had met since her father's passing. She wanted to hug him but knew that it was pointless to try and form a connection with someone she was about to leave behind. Instead, she pushed the feeling aside as she had practiced for so many months.

"Since then," he continued, "I have been looking for some way to free them. I have to believe they are still alive, still waiting for me. Perhaps they have been put into service. Perhaps they are in the dungeon, but I know they're alive. I will find a way in, and we will be a family again." He finished his speech with a sullen look.

"Enough about me." He forced a smile, "Are you still planning on heading off to find a way home?"

"Considering I have no idea why I'm here, I suppose I'm going to try and figure that out. I suppose if I don't know where I'm going, it doesn't matter how I get there." She echoed the words she had heard the day before from Ches.

He packed her a small bag with a few things from the kitchen. She thanked him and said goodbye. It all seemed more formal than she would have liked, but since relaying his story Thomas seemed more distant than he had the day before. She regretted pushing him but chalked it up to Murphy's Law where she and boys were concerned. As she walked away, Thomas hollered for her to stop, making her heart skip a beat. Rushing toward her, he placed a small purse of coins in her hand. "Look… if you're going into the forest, you may want more provisions," he said. "Start at the Baker, they have... amazing cinnamon buns." He gave her directions to find the mysterious baker, and she wondered a little at his obsession with cinnamon buns as she attempted to take in the instructions. Still, she was never one to turn down a good pastry. She tucked the purse away and nodded her thanks.

"Oh! Wait! I almost forgot!" Thomas ran back into the house and returned with a small item in his hand. When he was close enough, she could tell it was her phone. Obviously, he didn't understand it was of no use to her anymore. Still, it was nice of him to remember she had forgotten it. When he was once again next to her, he handed her the dead weight. Instead of a lifeless mass, however, the screen was lit. The bars in the top were gone, replaced by the words no services, but the rest of the tiny boxes were lit. The battery was full. Alex looked up at Thomas, unable to hide the shock on her face.

"I like to tinker." His smile from yesterday returned, as he seemed to revel in her pleasure. "Of course," he smiled down at her, "if you change your mind, I'll be here to help you get settled." He placed his hand on her shoulder and awkwardly rubbed it averting direct eye contact. Alex stifled a giddy giggle and hid her smirk as she turned to walk in the direction Thomas had indicated.

# HOT CROSS BUNS

The dirt streets of the outer districts were as Alex remembered from the day before. They grew more deliberate and were replaced with cobbles as she came closer to the wall. The architecture also morphed from wood and mud structures to taller and larger stone houses. Clearly, even among the poor, there were class divisions. The wall stood ominously between her and what she now knew to be The Park. It was tall enough that you couldn't see the towering spires that lay beyond. Flashing images of terrifying and dark creatures appeared on the screens, floating against a forested backdrop. They snarled and tore the flesh off the digital representations of city dwellers venturing too close to the timberland. New images appeared and disappeared in flashes. They showed people being ripped to pieces by ghoulish creatures and screaming terrified children being chased by spirits. The pictures were almost too graphic for her to watch, and she'd seen many a horror film back in her world. The speed of the images changing was enough sensory overload for her to avert her eyes.

The streets became cleaner as she entered what she correctly assumed was the market based on Thomas' directions. Various shops lined the streets, each with a wooden sign showing its contents. A few of them had carts out front, piled high with goods. The market appeared to have everything from food and beverage to clothing and furniture. The only thing it lacked was the presence of an electronics store. Residents buzzed about picking up provisions. A woman walked past, followed by a glowing orb, similar to the one from the previous day. This one, however, had bags suspended from its underside. Another woman flipped her hand back, and a list appeared on the underside of her forearm. She had no screen, and the information was displayed directly on her skin. She tapped one of the boxes beside an item she had just bought, and a bright green check appeared. When she returned her hand to its relaxed state, the list disappeared, and she moved to the next stall.

Scanning the crowd Alex contemplated who might know where the infamous *Oothro* might be. She saw one young man, about the age of Thomas' father in the photo, stacking some bread on a table out in front of a bakery. Remembering Thomas' advice, she figured it was as good a place as any to start.

"Excuse me?" she tried to sound and look like she fit into the crowd. Out of the corner of her eye, she could see a black armored guard patrolling the perimeter of the market along the wall, and she shivered.

"What can I get for ye lass?" His accent was like those from Scotland or Ireland in her world. When he finally looked away from his work and down at her, he stepped back in surprise. His composure was only lost for seconds, however, and he looked around nervously before he continued with the transaction. "Perhaps we have what you're looking for inside." His voice rose over the hum of the busy crowd. A few residents looked over but soon returned to their tasks. The statement seemed more like a recommendation than a request, and she hadn't even asked for anything.

"Well," Alex continued. She wanted to be in and out of the market as fast as possible. If she was going to find this mysterious man with answers, something told her she had to be quick. She also had no desire to meet with the guards again. "I was hoping for some information actually. Do you know an *Oothro?*" The man glanced at the guard across the square.

"Hot Crossed Buns you say?" he said a bit louder than he needed. "Why yes! We have those... inside." He emphasized the last word. Instead of waiting for her to respond, he walked through the door, not looking back. His apron was coated with flour and other baking ingredients, and when he turned around, she could see an equal amount of baking dust on the back of his dark pants. It was as if he rolled around in the stuff. The smell of fresh baking had already been wafting from the shop, and it intensified ten fold as he opened the door. The smell of cinnamon buns and chocolate chip cookies met her with delightful dancing in her nostrils. The inside of the shop matched the man's garments. The floor, tables, and walls were covered in flour, and a woman busied herself kneading some dough on a table toward the back. Despite the mess, everything looked like it was perfectly divine to eat. The baskets of buns, browned to a golden shine, had been glazed with butter. Rolled pastries, filled with meat, were stacked on a wicker platter. It was still early in the day, and Alex assumed they must have just opened for business. Other residents began to trickle in, placing various wares in their baskets. A few more patrons had glowing orb helpers following them, and she made a mental note to try and find one for herself.

The man took her to the back counter, where the woman was steadily kneading dough. She didn't seem to be paying attention to the task she performed. Instead, her eyes wandered over the crowd, watching for what Alex could only assume were thieves or people needing help. As they approached, the woman noticed them and turned. She eyed Alex up and down before raising her eyebrows.

"Not from around here, are ya?" she smirked before returning her attention back to her table. Alex shifted uncomfortably. How had the woman known? She was wearing the clothes Thomas set out, she hadn't even opened her mouth yet. Noticing her confusion, the woman continued. "Look around lass, what do you notice about every person here?"

Alex scanned the room. It was filled with market goers of all shapes and sizes. Not one of them looked like the other. Each of them seemed to have their mind set on a specific task, and none seemed to pay attention to the others aside from polite greetings and asking people to excuse their reach. They all wore clothes similar in style to her. Most of them, however, wore muddy leather boots, the bottoms of their pants and dresses stained with many days of use. The realization hit her like a punch in the gut. She looked down at her own garment. It was in pristine condition. Many days of disuse, locked away in a drawer, meant that they were as clean as the day they were made. She shifted, a bit embarrassed at her lack of preparedness. Why hadn't Thomas said anything? Her frustration was only allowed to percolate for a second before her thoughts were interrupted.

"She was asking about... *Oothro.*" The man whispered the last word like it was a secret that only the two of them knew.

"Hm." The woman pursed her lips together. "Was she?" There

was a pause before the woman continued. She returned to kneading, no longer concerned with the people busying themselves with purchases. The man, however, had less composure. He shifted nervously from one foot to the next, scanning the crowd. "And how might you have come across a name like that?" the woman asked, continuing to work her hands into the dough.

It was Alex's turn to shift uncomfortably. Thomas had been so kind to her, she wasn't sure if she should bring him into the conversation. After all, perhaps the two people she had questioned were in league with the Queen. Why hadn't she observed for longer before approaching someone?! At least, she would have noticed the difference between her clothing and the rest. She cursed herself while trying to decide what to say. The man seemed genuinely concerned that someone would hear them, which didn't make her feel any more at ease about their situation. She began to wonder what was so special about Oothro.

"Well?" the woman prodded again, waiting patiently for a response.

"I…" Alex hesitated for a final moment before asserting herself, "A friend of mine told me that Oothro could help me get home, or, at least, tell me why I'm here."

"A friend eh? And does this friend of yours have a name?"

"My friend's name is of no concern," she feigned confidence. "Do you know where to find him or not? If not, I'll move on."

The woman stopped what she was doing, and one eyebrow made its way to her hairline. "You expect us to trust you, yet you won't extend the same?" She returned to her task. "Well I suppose if you feel you can get the information you look for elsewhere, you're welcome to go. I would be a bit warier about who you approach in the future. We aren't all as… welcoming."

Alex pursed her lips together. The stubborn part of her was about to kick in; the one that always seemed to arrive when she and her mother started to have any conversation at all. She pushed her breath through her nostrils before she spoke, "Thomas, his name is Thomas." She glared at the woman like a child who had just been relieved of a toy.

"See? Was that so hard?" The woman stopped her work and walked toward the back of the shop to a small door. "Follow me," she called over her shoulder. They left the man behind, ringing his hands as they disappeared into the back room.

# BEDROLLS AND BACKPACKS

The room they entered was a small pantry. Sacks of flour, grains, and spices were piled neatly along the back wall along with a few barrels. They were covered with dust from years of disuse. The woman locked the door behind them, and Alex panicked. She jiggled the handle furiously.

"That will be quite enough, do you want to attract attention?" the woman scolded. Walking across the room to a shelf of recipe books, she tugged at one. As it tilted out of its spot, a small hiss of pressure releasing came from the corner of the wall beside the barrels. The left wall, which Alex just noticed remained empty, slowly and silently moved open.

Behind the wall lay a much different sight than the one she had just left. Everything was clean and put in place. Several machines, like the one she had seen the woman using when the guard was chasing her, were lined up on a counter. Each was silently working, kneading the dough in their bowls, periodically adding ingredients. Now that she was closer, she could see that each of them had a different shaped pan in front of it. One of them finished kneading, and the bowl tilted, dumping the bread into the pan. The woman placed towels over the pans that awaited attention and moved them to another counter with a conveyor. She busied herself around the room, adjusting pans of baked goods. When she had finished her work, she went to a black slab in the corner and ordered two cups of tea. Sitting at the island in the center of the room, she finally motioned for Alex to sit.

They sat in silence for a few long minutes. Alex wasn't sure what to do next? All she wanted was to find out where Oothro was, and now she was having tea, in the secret back room of a bakery, with a cryptic woman, who quite frankly wasn't very friendly.

"Well?" the woman broke the silence.

"Well, what?" Alex was puzzled.

"You're the one with questions, dearie," the woman said flatly. Her demeanor softened as she drank her tea. The absence of prying eyes seemed to put her at ease. As much as she wanted to know about Oothro, Alex's curiosity about the room was greater. The woman clearly had a replicator in the corner, and they had gone to so much trouble to hide their secret room full of the latest technology.

"Why don't you just use the replicator to make your bread?" Alex blurted. The unfamiliar surroundings and constant introduction to new situations were beginning to put her on edge. She felt like she was back in school, and the awkwardness she displayed there was beginning to shine through.

"You came all this way to ask me about my baking practices?" The woman half chuckled, and Alex shrank down. Instead of responding, the woman went over to the replicator and ordered a small cinnamon bun. She cut it into pieces and offered one to Alex. The first bite was delightful. It reminded her of cinnamon buns at the mall, the ones that she tried hard to resist every time she walked through their intoxicating scent bubble. After she had finished a few bites, the woman placed another piece in front of her. This one was from the rack of cooling items next to the ovens. In contrast, the flavor was divine. The explosion of cinnamon and sugar in her mouth instantly relaxed her. She forgot, for a moment, where she was, and what she was trying to do. Instead, she lost herself in a pocket dimension of flavor. She didn't realize how bland and stale the first one tasted until this one was in her mouth. Seeing Alex's realization, the woman placed the rest of the bun on a plate in front of them and removed the other.

"Now that we've settled that," the woman broke Alex's trance. "You were asking about finding something?"

"Someone actually. Oothro; I want to find Oothro."

"I'm surprised Thomas didn't tell you to be more careful when asking about Oothro." Alex tensed. She hadn't wanted to mention Thomas, and now it seemed as if he was already connected in some way.

"Calm down," the woman answered Alex's silent protest, "I'd recognize that outfit anywhere. Leniva was one of my greatest friends." The woman paused for a moment in silent reflection before continuing.

"Not everyone in this city is willing to sit back and let the Queen oppress them. There is a resistance, and it grows larger with every passing season. Thomas' parents were part of the group that wanted to lead us to rise up. I resisted for quite some time, but when they were taken, we knew we needed to at least help where we could. Since then we've been the information hub for the rebellion. We send them new candidates and they ensure that we stay well hidden."

"Resistance?" It all sounded very glamorous, but Alex had no desire to join a rebellion. She could hardly stand up to the kids at school, what use would she be to a group of rebels? Not that she was in a rush to get home either, but she needed answers. Once she had those, perhaps she could find a small cabin in the woods where she could live her life out in peace and harmony, no one else around to needle her. "I... well you see... I just wanted to find Oothro. I'm sorry if you thought..."

"Oh don't worry child, you likely wouldn't even pass initiation, I was only providing context."

"Oh," Alex couldn't help but feel hurt even though she had no desire to join. What did that mean, she wouldn't even pass initiation? Her chest puffed with stubborn pride, "Well... right. As I said, I didn't want to join the silly rebellion anyway."

The woman gave a knowing smile and continued, "Finding *Oothro* won't be as easy as you think. I can give you a map. It will lead you to a place deep in the wood, where the mountains meet the trees, and the scorched earth ends. Our map is old. There are pieces missing, but if your search is pure, all will become clear when you need it to. The forest is dangerous. There are patrols through most of the outer forest, and you'll need at least two days' travel by foot to get there. Once you're there, you'll find the entrance to a cave. *Oothro* can be found inside." There was something about the way the woman said Oothro that didn't seem quite right. She emphasized and slowed her speech over the name each time she said it.

"Thank you. I'm ready." Alex said with more confidence than she felt. The woman nodded and walked over to a table that had been turned into a makeshift desk in the corner of the room. She rifled through a few items before emerging with her prize. She handed over a small tablet. The screen was cracked and pixelated lines ran through it when she turned it on.

"It's the only spare I have." The woman apologized. As the screen illuminated she could see that some of the map was missing as if the file had been corrupted somewhere along the way. There was a path leading from the city into the forest toward a hilly region. A cave stood out amongst the features, but just before the cave a large chunk of the image was missing.

"What's supposed to be here?" she pointed to the void space she assumed held vital information.

"I have never made the journey myself. I can't tell you what you might find. All I can tell you is to be cautious. Find the cave and you'll find what you seek." The woman was polite but final in her words, and as if sensing Alex's discomfort continued. "I was merely noticing how ill prepared you were to spend two days in the forest, but that can be fixed. Clearly, Thomas never thought of that before sending you on your way. She walked over to a cupboard. As it opened, Alex could see that it housed various dishes and utensils. The woman pulled at one of the spoons and the entire cupboard morphed before her eyes. It looked like something from a movie as the shelves flipped and disappeared, the back of the cabinet opening, providing another entrance to a small room. Inside, there were various supplies, packs, ropes, and pouches, and the woman pulled a shoulder pack from the wall and handed it to Alex. It was empty, and Alex placed the small pouch of coins Thomas had given her in it next to the map.

"Okay, so here's a cloak," the woman said, holding out a deep green garment to Alex. It was already weathered, perhaps by design. "It should keep you warm and dry."

Alex took the cloak gratefully, the rough material feeling reassuringly sturdy in her hands. "Thank you," she said, slipping it over her shoulders and fastening it at the neck.

The woman nodded, her expression serious. "You'll need a bedroll too," she said, handing Alex a tightly rolled bundle. "And some food. I've got some dried meat, hardtack, and a few apples here that should last you a few days."

Alex accepted the supplies, stuffing them into her small pack. "I really appreciate this," she said, looking up at the woman. "I don't know what I would have done without your help.

The woman had chuckled when Alex saw a glowing orb among the pile of supplies and excitedly asked if she could bring one. Shrugging, the woman agreed; obviously thinking the tool was useless for this type of trip. Alex wasn't particularly fond of camping, too many creepy crawlies, and the longer she spent in this room, the more she felt like she was in for an uncomfortable few days. At least she'd be out of the city and away from all this craziness. Even if she didn't find the elusive Oothro, perhaps she would find that quiet place to escape and hide from everyone in this world and her own.

Once the woman was satisfied with Alex's state of preparedness, they made their way back out to the main bakery. Customers still bustled around, selecting cakes and buns for the evening meal. No one noticed the girl with the bedroll. With a nod and a smile, Alex left the bakery and headed deeper into the city.

# HOW COULD SHE...

Alex's mind was reeling. As she stepped cautiously from one shadow to the next, avoiding eye contact wherever possible, she observed the people surrounding her. Everyone seemed to be followed by a cloud of depression. From time to time, they would cast a smile in greeting, but as soon as they passed each other, their faces would return to their normal sullen state. As she poked herself between two houses, she caught a glimpse of the same android from the day before. He held his arm out in front of him, and a glowing clock face with ticking hands hovered above it.

"Oh dear oh my, I'm late again," the voice coming from the strange robot reminded her of C3P0. With no one to distract her this time, she followed the bot along the road, careful to stay out of sight. Most of its body was covered in a solid white alloy that cast a glare from the sun. The gears were only visible through the clear window on each limb, chest and back. They ticked away inside him, a methodical rhythm like a heartbeat guiding their movement. The words of his chant never changed. He seemed very concerned about the time, and he never looked up from his path. The most peculiar thing was how the others in the city reacted to him. All of them moved out of his way immediately without a word, some of them panicked as they dragged their children to the side of the road and hurried them along after he had passed. Some muttered to each other in whispers as he moved past them while others seemed to shake their heads in sadness or regret like they had lost a cherished family member. Consistently, however, they each took notice and responded. The further along the path Alex followed, the more curious she became until they finally reached a spot where the buildings seemed vacant, and the streets were practically void of activity. Her attention was taken so deeply that she had barely noticed the slow degradation in quality of the building surrounding her as they had walked. This new section of the city was filled with broken and burnt houses, most of them half collapsed. The android made his way to the only opening in the wall that Alex had seen since the day began. Beyond, she could barely make out a green lawn and flowerbed surrounding one of the tall buildings she had seen from the edge of the city. The image was blurred as the gap between the walls emitted some form of a shield, or heat signature reminiscent of heat waves on a warm summer day. Trance-like, Alex walked toward the blurred opening.

She was so involved in her observation of the mechanical man that she had missed the guards standing on either side of the gate. The second she came close, a hydraulic clicking noise disrupted her thoughts. Both guards stood, arms outstretched, daring her to come closer. Flashes of the previous day rose in her memory, and she backed away. The ticking of the mysterious mechanical man had made her oblivious to her other surroundings. Now that she was paying attention, for the first time, she noticed a line of stockades facing the wall to the right of the guards. They had been hidden by the broken buildings when she approached.

The guards lowered their weapons as soon as she backed away. As she moved toward the line of prisoners, however, the guards immediately noticed her again. This time, the sound of their weapons powering up was unmistakable. Clearly, any patience they had was wearing thin. Once again, Alex backed up until she was out of sight. A shiver rose from her as she absorbed the scene. She had heard of medieval torture and punishment, but the stories were nothing compared to what she saw in front of her. Lines of prisoners, at least two dozen by her count, were locked with head and hands in a metal contraption resembling a stockade. The edges were angular and sharp, and each bore the symbol of a spade.

The prisoners ranged in age from about nine to extremely eighty-nine, each with ragged and gaunt silhouettes. Some of them had given up on standing all together, their bodies hanging limp. Whimpering and crying was the norm among the group, which no one around seemed to pay any attention to. Those who ventured into the streets around the area deliberately avoided looking in the direction of the captives. Almost all of them had defecated and urinated on themselves, and it was clear that no one had taken any care to tend to them for quite some time. Some seemed fresher than others as if the group had grown over time. A few new stockades had been erected and stood empty while a small robot pulled materials from its attached trailer and continued to build more of them beside the rest. The worst part about the scene was the horrific images being cast on the wall in front of them. The whole thing reminded her of sensory stimulation torture she had once regretted stumbling across during an internet search. *Why has no one stopped this?!*

The youngest captive also seemed to be the freshest. Her red cloak hung down around her shoulders, so that its weight pulled back and choked her slightly. Tears streamed down her face, and her dress was stained with several days of urine. Her clothes were still relatively crisp considering. She was standing on a box to allow her head to fit nicely into the bonds that held her. Clearly these were simple folk, and some of them likely had no clue how to stop it, but according to her Intel from only hours ago, there was a resistance movement. Surely this had to be high on their list of priorities. If it wasn't, then the Queen must be even more horrific than Alex imagined.

If no one else was going to do something, Alex felt she must. There was a control panel on the wall three feet away from the guards. If she went close to the prisoners or the gate, she would be vaporized instantly. There had to be some way she could distract them. Alex thought about her options for a few moments before settling on the only thing she thought might stand any chance of success. Pulling out the small floating orb, she looked closely at it to see if there was any way to open it. At first, the smooth surface seemed to have no seams at all. In the right light, however, she managed to see the tiny hairline crack. Twisting and prying, she worked at it for twenty minutes before it gave way. She wasn't even sure what she would do with it once she got it open, but it wasn't the first time she tore apart something to see how it ticked. She wagered that a glowing orb on its own wouldn't be enough to draw the guards away from their post. Alex's head ached as the whimpering rose and fell behind her. She had turned her back to the group as she sat between two abandoned homes. In this position, the visual stimulation was removed, but the high-pitched humming, loud crashing music, and various animal noises that were piped alongside the music was enough to make her go crazy all on its own. God knows how broken the poor people in the stocks were by this time. The longer she sat, working away at the orb, the more furious she became at this mysterious Queen that everyone feared. *How could anyone be so cruel? What could a nine-year-old do that would land her in such torment?!*

Once the ball was in two pieces, Alex could see how the mechanisms worked inside. She wasn't sure how the anti-gravity worked, as there didn't appear to be any fans or motors manipulating the air, but she assumed that the small black cube in the center had something to do with it. A small light shone from a bulb at the top of the ball, which Alex assumed gave it light-up properties. The question that lingered was how to use this to distract the guards. For a split second, she thought it might be easier to simply light a building on fire, but she wasn't sure how fast a fire like that would spread and it would be too dangerous if she wasn't able to figure out how to free the captives.

Her phone buzzed in her pocket, letting out a loud ding at the same time. Luckily, the sound was drowned out by the noise from the screen. Alex pulled out the phone and was confused. She never received texts from anyone, and she hadn't had service earlier, yet there it was, a lone text waiting for her. It still said no service, yet it began to buzz and ring again, and again, and again. A plethora of texts began flooding in. When she finally managed to fumble it out of her pocket and silence it, she had already received at least twenty texts. They continued for about five minutes before her phone was once again silent. Alex stared, dumbfounded at the words that lay in front of her, since she didn't have anyone but family in her phone's contacts, none of the numbers were recognized. They were all different. At least two hundred messages waited for her.

Thinking of you.

I'm sorry for everything I
ever said to make you
sad.

Comas suck. Wake up.

You probably won't know
y u have so many texts
when u wake. The
teachers thot u could use
sum engorgement. I thot
I'd send a text to say u
aren't alone, they really
bug me too.

We were told this would
be anonymous... did you
really jump? That makes
me think you're brave. If
you do wake up, maybe
we can be brave
together and stand up to
them.

I didn't know you were so
sad, I'm sorry for
laughing along.

I miss seeing your face
in the hall.

Tears streamed down Alex's face as she scanned the messages.

The memory of the moments before waking in Wonderland had come flooding back with the reminders from her classmates. Flashes of Tasha, her gang, and the laughter following her once again out of the schoolyard cut her heart as much as they had the first time. Her eyes blurred as she ran that day, and she didn't see the car as she ran across the street. She didn't remember feeling anything. She was simply staring at the grill hurtling toward her, and then the next thing she remembered was waking in Wonderland.

The realization made everything seem imagined and real at the same time. Puzzling over the messages she realized that at least she wasn't dead. The texts were telling her to wake up and that she was in her own world, lying in a coma. So, is this all a dream? However, the texts seemed to be coming through in real time, meaning that there was something real about this world. For the first time, she had some desire to leave this all behind and return to her own world. Even though she knew how she had been brought here, she still wanted answers. Why had she been brought here? Every coma patient can't end up in Wonderland, or there would be a lot more *new* people all the time. Was this an alternate reality? Was her consciousness transferred to a new plane when she was hit? If she died, would she stay in Wonderland, or be transported somewhere else? She didn't want to find out. A high-pitched squeal coming from the screens behind her pulled her out of her trance. She wiped the tears from her face and stared down at her phone. The idea finally solidified itself in her mind. She pressed the screen until her images came up, and she selected a picture of herself, taken at her last birthday, standing in the middle of the yard.

Hours passed as she tinkered. Nothing seemed to work right at first, but her father's voice in the back of her mind "try something new" and "buck up, no scientific discoveries were made in one session." came to mind. It took her almost eight hours of taking things apart and putting them back together again before she finally understood how this weird foreign technology worked. It was similar to the projection technology they had used in science class a few times. Finally, she had the image of herself projecting as a full-size projection in front of the ball. She sealed the ball again and using a small knife she found in her pack, she made a hole for the light and projection to escape. Unfortunately, this meant that her phone would be lost to her, but it was a sacrifice she needed to make for the suffering people waiting behind her. Part of her felt that freeing them would be a small victory that she could never have had in her own world. The orbs were used for carrying heavy loads as well, so the extra weight did little to affect the ball's flight. Setting it off in the direction of the guards, she waited for them to respond.

As she had expected, the guards had trouble discerning one human shape from the next. They were machines, and their programming obviously wasn't very sophisticated. The image the ball projected was solid enough to hide the ball as it approached, and the guards raised their arms in protest. When the human figure continued forward, blue lights pulsed out of their guns. A few stray blasts almost grazed the orb, but it managed to complete its course unscathed. Once it crossed the barrier, it had deactivated and rolled off the path before the guards could swivel and understand what had happened. To them, it looked as if the girl had escaped into The Park district, and they pursued, leaving their post unguarded.

Alex knew she wouldn't have much time before they returned. She sprinted toward the control panel on the wall. Catching her breath, she let her eyes wander over the panel. The set of numbers and symbols made no sense. She began by trying buttons, but when it was apparent that she was causing more pain than relief to the waiting citizens she felt a different approach was warranted. She scanned the edges, looking for some weakness. Reaching to her pack, she once again freed the small knife. The cover to the control panel popped off easily, its engineer obviously thinking no one would attempt to get inside. A maze of circuits mixed with glowing microchips and gears greeted her. It was the oddest combination of parts she had ever seen. The gears and wires came to life in front of her eyes, and an imaginary blueprint that only she could see floated just in front of the actual circuit board. As far back as she could remember, examining mazes had been a family game for Alex. They would spend hours huddled around a table, tracing every twist and turn, trying to find where each wire led. It was a challenge that Alex had always enjoyed, one that had honed her attention to detail and her ability to solve complex puzzles. As she got older, Alex's interests had shifted to computer circuit boards, which presented an even greater challenge. With hundreds of tiny components and intricate pathways, it was like a digital labyrinth waiting to be solved. To Alex, it was more than just a game. It was a way of life, a testament to her perseverance and determination to succeed no matter how daunting the task. They had done it so often, that when Alex scanned each path, it was easy to see which chip connected to which circuit. The easiest solution would be to smash the controls. However, that could leave the prisoners stuck in their restraints, which would serve no one in the end. No, she had to figure out which ones worked each button. One circuit snaked off toward the screen in front of the captives. That one would turn off the wall. Two more winding pathways led downward. She assumed one of them would be the stockade controls, but she had no way to tell for sure without trying. Carefully, she replaced the panel, so the buttons were positioned over their respective triggers. Pressing the button, she knew would make the screen respond, she watched as it blinked off. At first, the prisoners didn't notice, but after a few seconds of silence even those that had closed their eyes began to open them. Everyone was staring at her; some already trying to muster their strength to run.

The next two buttons were going to be a gamble. She had no way to predict what would happen, or if pressing them would even release the prisoners. For all she knew, the release could be on each individual manacle. Her finger hesitated over the button on the right for a split second before settling on it and pressing it. Her head whipped around as screams erupted to her right. Knees buckled as electricity bounced from one person to the next, a sheet of electricity connecting each of the stocks, coursing through her awaiting appendages. The surprise of it made her finger linger longer than it should have, and the youngest girl buckled. She hesitated. Who knew what horrors and torture the Queen had built into her open prison. There had been no way to predict the first horror. She closed her eyes, wavering. Footsteps grew closer from the other side of the wall. The guards were returning to their posts. Pressing the second button, she let out the breath she had been holding. Simultaneously, she heard some clicking noises and the bars that had been holding the group's hands and heads in place receded into the stockades. A few newly released prisoners bolted. Others stood there for a few moments, disoriented, and confused about their new situation. When they were sure it wasn't a cruel trick of the Queen to give her opportunity to inflict more pain, they too found their legs and ran off, some limping, some hobbling, but all going as quickly as they could. None of them stopped to help their fellow prisoners, all seemed extremely fearful for their own lives. Only one remained: a small figure, lying on the ground, a tiny girl, whom Alex had shocked into unconsciousness.

Alex ran to the girl, kneeled, and rolled her over, resting the girl's delicate head in her lap. She looked over her shoulder, watching for the guards as she tried desperately to revive the girl. There was still a pulse, for which Alex was relieved. She couldn't live with herself if she'd killed the girl, accidentally or not. Alex shook the child, each shake becoming more furious than the last as Alex grew increasingly sure the guards would be on them at any moment. Finally, the girl's eyes fluttered open. Confusion showed in her eyes, then fear.

"Shhh," Alex comforted. "It's okay. You're free now, you're safe." The girl didn't respond. Tears began to stream down her face, and she rolled over, reaching her arms around Alex and burying her face in Alex's stomach.

"We have to go, the guards will be here soon." The girl responded to Alex's nudge and they both got to their feet. Just as they stood, a laser sounded from behind them and a beam hit the ground, making it sizzle and smoke. Alex was sure the shot was meant to land exactly where it had as a warning. Grabbing the girl's hand, she darted, pulling the girl with her. A few more shots flew past them, a little too close for comfort, making her think that their warnings were over. They wound their way between the buildings, guards in pursuit. Anyone on the street was soon cowering in their own corner, trying to avoid stray fire, or rushing inside buildings. She turned around for a split second and saw a stray beam disintegrate a bystander into dust. Alex knew they had to get far enough away before finding a hiding spot. If the guards spotted them, even for a split second, as they entered a building, or ducked into a corner, they would be trapped, and all would be lost. She urged the child to run faster, but the girl had been in the same standing position for so long, Alex suspected she was moving as fast as she could, even if adrenaline was coursing through her. When Alex thought they were a safe enough distance, she ducked into a burnt-out building, pulling the girl into the far corner, and urging her to be as quiet as she could.

Hidden by the shadows, they crouched silently behind the crumbling brick wall, peering through the gap in the missing door as the guards patrolled the street. Every step they took was deliberate, cautious, as if they knew their quarry was close by. The fugitives held their breath, hearts pounding in their chests as the guards slowed down, scanning the surrounding buildings for any sign of movement. In the stillness of the night, the sound of their boots hitting the pavement echoed like gunshots. The girl's breathing was finally slowing, but the fugitives knew they couldn't let their guard down. The guards would be back shortly, circling around like sharks, waiting for their prey to slip up and leave their hiding place too soon. Alex gritted her teeth, determined not to give them the satisfaction of capturing them. She clutched her makeshift weapon tightly, ready to fight if necessary. The next few minutes would determine their fate. They both held their breath and the guards eventually made their way past. After they seemed far enough away, she turned to the girl.

"I'm Alex," she whispered quietly to the girl when the guards were far enough away. She hoped that the offering would help calm the child.

"I'm Olivia." The girl's voice was barely a whisper.

"Hi, Olivia. It's going to be okay you know. They will give up soon enough." She tried to reassure the girl, but she wasn't so sure herself. As she finished the sentence, the sound of boots on rocks came from outside. The guards appeared once again on the street, clearly visible through the door opening. Alex raised a finger to her lips and the girl cowered against Alex's chest. After a few moments, they once again disappeared back toward the stocks.

"Olivia, why were you locked up?" Alex realized that the choice of conversation wasn't that pleasant, but she was too concerned to just leave the matter unknown. The girl hung her head, as a toddler would when they were asked who ate the last cookie. "It's okay, I'm sure whatever it is, it can't be as bad as you think."

"They found it. I was supposed to hide it, but they found it." The girl's voice was finally gaining volume, but it still barely registered as sound.

"Found what?" Alex encouraged.

"Mom and Dad said not to show anyone, that it was only for talking to them. They went on a trip. They said they would be back in a few weeks. The communicator was only supposed to be for emergencies."

"It's okay," Alex reassured, "You can tell me." The guards hadn't come back, but Alex wanted to be sure they had given up before they ventured back into the streets. At the very least, she would know a bit more about the girl she had risked her life to save.

"I was dumb, but the other girls were laughing, telling me we were too poor to have nice things. No one in the Cistern has nice things, but I wanted to prove to them that we could find tech too. I only pulled it out for a second when the patrols came. They saw me and grabbed me. I kept hoping mom and dad would be back soon, but they still haven't come. Maybe they'll never come." Tears once again welled in the girl's eyes. The scraping of heels could be heard once again, and this time, Alex could see the guards on the other side of the street. They were going in and out of each of the buildings. It would only be a matter of time before they would find the two of them, huddled in the corner.

"Listen." Alex asserted herself, forcing the girl out of self-pity. "I'm certain your parents are doing everything possible to come back. I'm sure they love you. They may be delayed, but I'm sure they'll be back." She paused. "I need you to stay here. Wait five minutes, then you run. You go as fast as you can, find your way home, and stay there for a few days. Don't look back, don't hesitate, just run…." The girl stared blankly. "Do you understand me?" Alex gave the girl a little shake. The guards were getting closer. Olivia's small head nodded, tears forming zebra stripes down her face. With final confirmation, Alex sprang into action.

She was out the door and onto the street before the guards were, ensuring they didn't know where she had come from. With any luck, she could force both of them to pursue her. When they stepped into sight, she let out a loud whistle, causing both of them to swivel their heads one hundred and eighty degrees. Alex shivered at the sight before bolting in a direction away from Olivia. The thought of being captured weighed heavily on her mind, and the reality of it becoming a certainty seemed to seep into her bones. Each breath became more labored, as if dragging weights of doubt from within her. A wave of exhaustion was washing over her, yet her pursuers' hunger for victory only seemed to grow stronger with each step they took closer to her. She could feel their determination closing in on her like a fog, leaving no escape route or hope of survival. They were heavy and methodical in their movements, but they were still fast enough to catch up. As the streets became more navigable, the rubble on the roads did less and less to deter them. The area she had stepped into was just as rundown, but far more populated than the destroyed part she had escaped from. The people here seemed to have grown used to the guards' presence, though there remained an air of resigned acceptance rather than defiance. Garbage littered the streets and stained structures, but it was obvious that life went on in this corner of the city. The congested street was soon a liability to her. She pushed at people, trying to get them to move out of her way, but it didn't take long after that for the guards to catch up. Once they were in striking distance, Alex braced for the lethal blow that would end her visit to Wonderland for good. Instead, cold hands grabbed each of her arms.

# STROLL IN THE PARK

The guards each wrapped a heavy metallic arm around hers, securing her and lifting her off the ground. The more she struggled, the tighter their grip became. People around her actively avoided eye contact as she was pulled back toward the gate where empty stocks lay waiting for fresh lawbreakers. She stared at her captors, heart racing in fear. If they weren't going to shoot her on the spot, it meant they had other plans for her, and she was afraid to imagine what they might be. Perhaps she would get to meet this elusive Queen. As they carried her through the streets, she searched for any sign of Olivia. She hid the pleasure on her face when she saw the edge of the young girl's cape around a dark corner, a small figure outlined in the shadows. At least, her sacrifice hadn't been in vain.

They walked through the gates, which brought them out of the claustrophobic alleys into The Park district. There was a stark change. The gloomy sky that had blanketed Wonderland since her arrival was replaced with a bright sunny, cloudless sky which Alex had to assume was a façade, since weather simply didn't work like that. The smell in The Park district was heavenly. It was a mixture of freshly cut grass, baking, and flowers. Each lawn that bordered a home was perfectly manicured. Alex stopped struggling as she took it all in. The closer she looked, the more it became evident that the grass and other vegetation was as synthetic as the grass she had landed on when she arrived. The people obviously still appreciated the beauty of plant life, since elaborate hedge animals covered their lawns.

The buildings were more magnificent up close than they had been from the edge of the city. Towering above, each floor seemed to be one room large, each glassed-in room simply stacked on top of the next. This left an incredible amount of room outside for people to walk, relax, and run. As it rose, each floor was offset slightly making the building spiral into the sky. While the buildings looked like glass, Alex couldn't see through most of the windows and noticed someone had taken great care to remove any stones nearby. Even the road appeared to be made of some special metal alloy, causing the boots of the guards to clank loudly as they tromped side by side through the streets. A few blocks later they halted. It appeared that even The Park didn't provide equal privileges. The guards' boots morphed and wheels protruding from their sides, allowing them to effortlessly glide along the smooth streets noiselessly.

The houses were taller and more elaborate the deeper she was dragged. Some of them had two or three spirals connected in the middle by glass walkways. The walkways were completely clear, and Alex could see people wandering through them on foot and some of them on floating chairs, strange goggles shielding their eyes. At the outer edges of The Park, there had been no one on the streets, but the crowds deeper in became viscous. Moving along like molasses in the street, their steady stream seemingly led by no purpose. Most of the residents didn't look up as the guards passed with their prize. Those that did, raised an eyebrow, sneered, or tilted their head curiously. None showed any compassion. Their clothing was bright and elaborate. Even the men wore frilled cuffs. The women wore corseted dresses, most in the same style she had come to recognize as the Queen's special uniform. Those that experimented with other styles kept the differences to a minimum, changing the length of skirt or amount of frill. The one thing that no one wore, however, was a smile. A feeling of discontent radiated from everyone around. The group shuffled their feet and avoided eye contact. Despite the air of superiority they conveyed when looking at her, they seemed resigned to the fact that the current situation was simply their best option.

The people who weren't walking around were either gliding on hover-like Segways or seated in chairs that floated without any external forces. Above them, soundlessly traveling along invisible streets, were small vehicular pods. They looked like shiny bullets with a dome over the top of them to house passengers. No that Alex observed seemed to be driving, some were reading from PCDs that hovered what looked like a daily newsfeed, some only stared ahead, and others wore goggles covering their eyes as they lounged back with odd grins plastered across their faces.

The residential areas gave way to streets with shops. These buildings looked more like the shops of her world, with architecture straight out of Victorian England. It was magnificent. If Alex had found this place in different circumstances, she would have spent hours wandering around, looking at the buildings and exploring shops. The windows were filled with every comfort imaginable. One shop sold the hover items that were prevalent everywhere she looked. Another window was filled with goggles in multiple colours. The caption read, *your real world awaits, the answer to your happiest moments.* Not all the stores sold technology. Some of them were filled with jewelry or jewel-encrusted household items. *Who needs a ruby covered dustpan?* Clothing stores lined an entire street, and another had a row of food vendors, each with a black stone cart to prepare anything requested. Alex's stomach protested in response, but she didn't think the guards would let her stop for a snack.

Finally, looming in front of her stood a grand castle. The main buildings were made of sturdy stone adorned with intricate carvings and embellishments. The carvings seemed to morph from the light and flowery feel of roses and flamingos to more ominous scenes where serpents were swallowing the flamingos headfirst. Its stones gave the impression they had been standing for centuries. Additions had been added that looked like the residences around the city. Stone turrets were intermingled with glass towers, and a grand drawbridge provided access to a courtyard. Several hovering green balls surrounded it with lenses on them, presumably surveillance. In place of the expected glass, energy fields occupied the windows, some displaying stained glass scenes that changed every few minutes. The area around the castle boasted actual vegetation, which was the first sign of real growth Alex had seen since arriving. Clear as a tropical ocean, the moat was tended to by small robots that hovered above the surface, periodically taking in some of the liquid and pushing it back out, likely filtered. Although the grass grew longer, it was still neatly trimmed, and the front wall was almost entirely covered with ivy.

Alex was lowered to the ground and permitted to walk, albeit with the guards still maintaining a firm grip on her. The courtyard was stark and simple, decorated in black and grey with a single obsidian spade fountain at its center. The interior was similarly mismatched, with old and seemingly futuristic items existing uneasily alongside each other, as if the retrofit had only been welcomed by half of those involved. The old tapestries were overlaid with new ones depicting the Queen. Most of them showed her wearing a divine circlet and revealing grand "modern" technologies. The primary tapestry in the entry hall was situated above massive, elaborately carved wooden doors that Alex assumed led to the throne room. It featured a set of interlocking rings glowing with yellow and orange fields. The rings looked as if they towered above the landscape as if they were cogs in a great machine. Each was connected to the other by a series of smaller cog like rings. The tapestry shimmered in the sun. It was one hundred percent fabric, yet the threads seemed to shift and buckle in the light, giving a sense of movement to the static image. In all her glory, the Queen stood in front of the rings proudly with her hands on her hips, smiling at the great accomplishment.

"Not a word." The command came from the guard on her left. Eerily humanlike, the voice made Alex jump away from the guard. She hadn't expected them to sound so... alive. Alex struggled against her unmoving robot shackles. They dragged her along, their wheeled feet making no sound on the hard stone of the castle floor. Stretching upward, the door to the main hall stopped just shy of the ceiling. Intricate designs were carved in it exalting Lindzel as the supreme savior of the land. Her worshippers were dressed in rich clothing and were shown enjoying the many life-altering inventions that she had introduced. Of course, even Alex knew that the discoveries had nothing to do with Lindzel. According to the stories Thomas told, Lindzel had an interest in ingenuity, but in the end, she had no real talent for it herself.

When they were close enough, the doors opened on their own.

# VERDICT

The entire room was filled with what Alex had expected to see in a castle. The center of the room was adorned with a lavish black and gold carpet that extended its entire length. Golden embroidered spades lining each edge of it. The stone floor flowed out from under it toward carved stone seating boxes. Some still showed remnants of the past ruler. The most prominent symbols and images were of hearts, and a short, pudgy woman playing croquet, using a flamingo as a mallet. A small mechanical robot with a large round ball for a body and another smaller ball perched on top for a head sent out a beam of light toward the mural. The scan lasted a few seconds as it recorded the entire panel and then proceeded to send a laser toward the stone, reshaping and carving it into a new design. The seats that lined the walls were on a series of platforms like an orchestra and each one was filled with colourful and boisterous versions of the woman in the carriage that had "welcomed" her to Wonderland. Alex felt the hair on her neck raise.

At the end of the room, a thin woman in a lacy black dress, sat on her throne. She paid no attention to the visitors to her court. Instead, she wore a set of strange goggles. They looked a lot like aviator goggles, lenses replaced with black glass. Alex couldn't tell if they were simply sunglasses or if they blocked out vision completely. A set of wires came out from the lenses and bore their way through the temples of the woman wearing them. It was as if they were an extension of her body and grew straight out of her temples into the device. The straps that held the goggles on moved toward her ears and a cushioned black earpiece. The strap continued around the back of her head and disappeared into her tangle of braids and hair, perfectly placed to accept the device.

The guards said nothing; they simply held her there in silence, which afforded Alex some time to examine the rest of the room. The similarities to what Alex expected of a castle stopped with the furniture. Halfway up the walls of the vaulted room, hundreds of screens connected side by side formed a glass wall of their own. Each optical rectangle showed a different scene, being broadcast from what seemed to be every section of the city. Some of the images showed locations that Alex had never seen before. There was a forested area, devoid of life for the moment as the camera panned around, searching or patrolling for something. Another screen showed a set of giant interlocking rings, each filled with a yellow energy field. The field pulsated from yellow to orange and back again. Each of the people in the seats was wearing goggles similar to those of the Queen, the ear coverings matching their outfits.

Behind her, a scuffle of feet could be heard on the carpet. She craned her head to see the white android from the marketplace bustling in. He continued to check the time using his PCD. As he approached, Alex could hear his mumbling become clearer.

"Oh dear oh my, I'm late again. She'll shut me down for sure this time. Shut it down. Pile of dust for certain." He paid no mind to the people around him. Instead, he simply moved up to the Queen's platform, cleared a spot on the table beside her and held his hand over it. A plate of biscuits and cup of tea appeared on the table. Then, nervously looking about, he ducked his head and bustled away toward the doors he had entered through. Alex turned to watch him go and a beam of blue light raced past her face, barely missing her. It did, however, hit its mark and the android disappeared into a pile of metallic dust on the floor in front of them.

"You're late," a cool and disturbing voice came from the direction of the throne. Alex turned to see the Queen standing, gun drawn and pointing in their direction. "Clean that up," she bellowed.

Two more identical androids made their way into the room. Their hands morphed into tubes, and they sucked up the bits of metal until nothing remained. As quickly as they could muster, they made their way out of the room mumbling to themselves, "Oh dear, oh my, oh dear," the entire way. All around, Alex could see the wires that were attached to each of the onlooker's temples detach and retract back into the devices that each of them wore. It was as if they had awoken from a trance or arrived home from a different world. Clearly, this wasn't a usual occurrence for them. They blinked as they came to the realization of where they were, most of them visibly annoyed at the interruption.

"Well… Well… Well." The voice remained cool as it punctuated each word. The Queen stepped down from her throne area onto the floor in front of Alex. The monarch was still looking down at her of course, but Alex could see that Queen Lindzel couldn't be more than twenty years old. Alex wrinkled her forehead; the timelines didn't add up.

"So, you're the new blood I've heard so much about."

Alex didn't respond.

"She thinks she's clever, brave, strong…," Lindzel addressed the crowd. Forced laughter rose among the group. Some were still annoyed that they had been summoned from their own little virtual worlds, but Alex could see that they made every effort to respond as expected when the Queen spoke. A single pointed finger wrapped on her forehead. "Hello in there, are you a mute?" Lindzel sighed as she took a step back, looking Alex up and down.

"Well, I suppose she could be. Judging from the icy glare, I'm assuming you can hear me." Lindzel started pacing back and forth in front of the throne. The silence was deafening. Alex could barely even hear them breathing. "So… hear this. I think you're pathetic. The fact that you've been able to even comprehend any of my ingenious gifts to this kingdom is sheer dumb luck. Perhaps a lifetime in the dungeons will help you understand." She paused again, circling around Alex, viewing her as if she was a prize show dog.

"Judging from your constitution, I don't expect you to last more than a few days. Perhaps you should end it now and save us all waiting. You hardly seem worth anyone's time." Lindzel reached into a chest beside the throne and pulled out a long rope. This time, the laughter that arose was awkward. She place the rope around Alex's neck, wrapping it a few times like a scarf.

"There, that should help." Then, turning to the guards she commanded, "put her in the cell with the beams." With one final look at Alex, a sneer spread across her face. She continued talking to the guards as she stared Alex directly in the eye. "She might need some knot lessons; be sure to show her the hangman's noose."

The scent of decay, past the point of body odor, rushed toward Alex as the Queen spun around and returned to her throne. The guards didn't move, waiting for the Queen to resume her previous activities. The goggles were replaced, and the small electrodes snaked their way to the woman's temples. Shuffling rose among the crowd as they whispered to each other quietly about what had just happened. Some of them immediately returned to whatever they were doing inside the goggles while others conversed quietly with their neighbors for a few seconds before becoming bored and joining their counterparts. Once everyone was back inside their own worlds, the guards turned her and dragged her from the room.

# INTO THE BELLY

Alex's feet dragged along the floor, making a slapping sound on the stone steps each time they dropped from one to the next. She had no desire to help the guards take her to her final resting place. The rest of the castle was a blur as the words repeated themselves over and over in her head. *You hardly seem worth anyone's time?* She had contemplated those words before. It was something she had heard a few times at school. Perhaps life would be easier in both worlds if she just ended it. It's not like she hadn't thought about it a hundred times anyway. If she died here, would she be sent back? Then what? She would be right back where she was when she left. A feeling in her gut, however, told her that the end was the end.

A heavy door squealed open, and a long corridor of cells lay before them. The scent of human decay and refuse assaulted her. Patrolling the single hallway were hovering drones. Their bodies were translucent and bubbled in the air like jellyfish underwater. Long tendrils flowed from their underside, each with a different purpose. Some had sharp quills on them, other barbs, and other long cylindrical tubes that mirrored gun barrels. Their pinkish blue hue almost made them beautiful if they didn't seem so deadly. The walls of the hallway were lined with cell doors. No bars were necessary, as the same glowing walls barred each prison. Alex's bag and other belongings were stripped off her and tossed in a pile near the doorway. Every so often a shock of electricity jumped out of the cell wall and onto the floor where they walked.

If the guard drones were terrifying, what Alex saw in each of the cells was horrific. She could smell them before she saw them. In some cells, lifeless bodies lay strewn across the floor. Some cells contained groups of people, huddled together, starved, all clearly dead. Other cells had people with strange contraptions attached to them, tied to beds with monitors connected to them. Every screen remained dormant and blackened. The dust on the monitors indicated that none of them had been used in a while. No one had cared enough to clean up the bodies, or even bury them. Of course, robots didn't have a sense of smell, so they had no idea how bad it really was. By the looks of things, no human guard had been down to the dungeons in a very long time, or they were more heartless than Alex had imagined. Was this what she was in for; days of relentless loneliness followed by inevitable starvation?

Her own cell wasn't empty. On the floor, a young woman lay rotting in the corner, the corpse was not yet dried out. Her ankles and wrists had metal straps around them, each with a canister attached. Her hands and feet were burned beyond recognition. A faint odor of burnt flesh still hung in the air. Any contents that remained in her stomach spilled out onto the floor.

Alex couldn't stop staring into the dead girl's eyes. Her face was bloated, and the body was beginning to expand. The sound of electricity buzzed as the cell was locked. The guards had taken the rope from her neck and at the last minute it was thrown at her, a noose already tied. She backed away from the body, running to the cell door, but stopped short, remembering what happened last time she had something contact the wall. She wasn't dumb enough to think her shoe trick would work here. These cells likely drew their power from the main city grid, meaning it would be more difficult to short them out. Unfortunately, all she had to look forward to now was a long wait.

Finding a tattered piece of fabric, she assumed was supposed to function as a blanket, she covered the body, careful not to disturb it since she had no desire to be covered with human bits if the body decided to explode. Ripping a piece of fabric from her shirt, she fashioned a mouth covering, filtering the smell of death. The only sounds that could be heard were her own. As far as she knew, she was utterly alone. She should have been used to it. *Wasn't this what she had longed for most days?* She would find a dark corner in the library, hoping that no one would find her over lunch, sitting in her cubicle, quietly eating her lunch. Strictly speaking, she wasn't supposed to eat her lunch in the library, but after a few reprimands, the librarians either gave up or took pity on her.

Placing her back against the wall, Alex slid to a sitting position and lightly banged her head against the stone wall. As with most of the city and Park district, the medieval-style dungeon had been retrofit with newer technology. There was no need for shackles when your prisoners couldn't even come close to escaping.

Her hand fell to the floor, resting on the rope that had been tossed casually in at her. Picking it up she caressed the tightly tied knot, feeling the rough spines along the soft pads of her fingers. She looked up to see if there was anything to fasten it to and sure to the Queens request thick beams ran across the ceiling. Now that she was motionless, her body felt the full brunt of her exhaustion. It was everything she could do to keep her head up. A steady drip of water could be heard from beyond her cage; reminding her of how parched she was. She chucked the rope across with what little strength she had left and watched it land next to her expired cellmate.

It was impossible to tell how many days went by, but Alex spent most of it curled up on the hard stone, not bothering to find a softer spot. Dirt and dust had accumulated on her face and was now streaked with veins caused by rivers of tears. She waited for some indication from the Queen, or anyone, that there might be an end to her loneliness. Alex shivered in the cold and rubbed their arms for warmth, but the icy chill seemed to seep into their bones. Her stomach had given up on growling with hunger.

As the silence enveloped her, Alex was left alone with her thoughts, the only company being the incessant drip she had heard on day one and the occasional scurrying of unseen vermin. She attempted to alter her activities to break up the boredom at first, pacing the cell, raging at her confinement by throwing anything she could find, screaming, crying, and collapsing in utter exhaustion.

Now, every action led her gaze back to the abandoned noose lying in wait on the floor, calling for her to end her own misery. No one checked on her. As far as she knew, she was forgotten the minute she left the throne room. When the feelings of sorrow and loss welled up inside her and she felt as if her heart would explode, she picked up the noose that lay on the floor.

The nearest thing within reach was the remains of some shackles bolted into the wall. A few logs had been thrown into the cell as seats or firewood. This might have indicated some show of compassion, though it didn't look like anyone in the dungeon lived long enough before being used as some experiment test subject. Her mind went to Thomas, and his hope of rescuing his parents, but judging from the state of the dungeon, they had died long ago. She felt sad for the friend she had almost had. With the noose in her hand, Alex struggled to work up the nerve. Hours went by as Alex sat staring at the rope in her hand.

Finally, she stood on a log that reminded her of something you'd find around a campfire. It was heavier than she expected, and the scraping noise it made on the dirty stone floor echoed through the corridor. She took one last look at the empty hallway, the experiment table in the cell across from her, and the hook on the wall before climbing onto the log and flinging the rope securely over the iron beam. She pulled it tight, tied it off, and gave it a few strong tugs. Her movements were slow and deliberate. As much as she felt this was her only course of action left, she wished or dared someone to see her, stop her.

The jellyfish drone hovered back and forth in the hallway soundlessly, occasionally passing her prison but paying no mind. The closer she came to carrying out her fate, the more determined she grew. She had thought about how she wanted to die plenty of times. Mostly, she had settled pilfering pills from the medicine cabinet at home. She had started by taking a small half-empty bottle of expired painkillers and had begun pilfering them from the stronger anti-depressants her mother had been prescribed. Then she had received her own prescription, which was easier than she thought it would be.

For several months, she had been hoarding them, doing extensive research about how much she would need to end it all, careful to do the research at the public library or school library. She feared what would come next, and she was scared about what it might feel like to die, which is why she had settled on pills in the end. A gun seemed messy, and her experience with them was in the digital world. Jumping off a building seemed like an over dramatic way to take your life, and she had no desire to make a spectacle of herself.

Options, however, were a luxury she no longer had. Judging from the corpses around her, she would starve and rot before she saw any signs of life anyway. No one even knew where she was, let alone cared enough to plan a grand escape effort. Placing the noose around her neck, she felt it scratch against the tender skin on her neck. Tears welled up in her eyes, blurring her vision. Through the blur, the familiar smile of her father came into view. His once inaudible voice was now resounding clearly in her ears.

*Alex no! You have more to do and so much more to live for.* Of course, her logic told her that her father wasn't here. He had left her behind. His voice merely reminded her that she wanted nothing but to be with him again. Her current course of action seemed to be the best way to achieve that.

She debated whether to jump off the log and snap her neck quickly, or whether to let her legs go slack and allow suffocation to take her consciousness. Her fingers were positioned between the rope and her skin. Her heart thudded in her ears. She took a deep breath and closed her eyes.

# AT THE END

Alarms sounded from beyond her vision. Her eyes shot open. There was a crash on the floor, sounding like metal on stone. She quickly removed the rope from her neck and jumped off the log to investigate, a sudden shot of adrenaline giving her the energy she needed.

"Alex!?" a male voice rang out, echoing along the walls. The sound of hurried footsteps filled the air. Alex stood frozen, wide-eyed, and confused. Who even knew where she was? The voice seemed familiar, but she couldn't place it.

"ALEX!?" The voice was more frantic.

Thomas appeared in front of her cell, his eyes matching hers in size. "Alex, I found you!?" He plunged toward the electric wall, causing it to shoot electric bolts toward him, knocking him backward.

Alex remembered what she had been in the middle of, what she had almost done. She couldn't speak or refused to speak. Either way, all she could bear to do was stare at the floor, refusing to make eye contact; embarrassed at what she had nearly been caught doing.

"Wait there. I'll be right back." Thomas ran back the way he had come. She heard the tromping of his feet and let out a sob. Nothing made sense anymore. She collapsed as a limp pile on the floor and covered her face. All the sorrow bottled up inside since she had lost her father poured out of her in torrents. She mourned her family, mourned her once-anonymous school experience, and mourned her sanity. She truly had descended into the depths of desperation, and someone she barely knew had almost witnessed it.

The familiar sound of the wall being deactivated barely registered before Thomas placed his hand on her shoulder.

"We have to go." His voice was soft and comforting, but still conveyed the urgency of the situation. Alex said nothing, but she stood and obeyed. Her pace grew faster to match his as he approached their escape route, and likely the way he had arrived. A drone lay broken into pieces on the ground, charred in places. She saw the gun dangling from his hand. In the floor, at the edge of the dungeon, a metal grate had been lifted. Human waste and water trickled into the drain. Alex wrinkled her nose and slowed as they approached.

"How did you find me? Why are you here?"

"I tracked you." His answer was a matter of fact. Clearly, he thought there were more pressing things to worry about than explaining his actions. He motioned for her to go down indicating that he would follow.

"Hurry." He urged when she hesitated. "The drone will have alerted the guards, if we're going to go, we have to go now!"

Alex lowered herself down into the dark tunnel as quickly as her body would allow. She had to crouch, and the smell was even stronger than in the dungeon, though she was almost grateful that the scent of rotting flesh was dissipating.

"Catch." Thomas hissed down. Her pack came flying at her seconds later. It fell through her hands and into the muck below. She had never been good at Catch. Thomas jumped down next to her, his boots splashing in the filthy water, but he made no indication of disgust. Reaching up, he lifted the grate back over the opening, careful not to drag it and scratch the stone floor, which would surely give away their position. Seconds after the grate made its way to its original resting place, the door to the dungeon flew open. Above them, they could hear the familiar sound of heavy metal boots on stone. There was another set of footsteps with them this time, softer and lighter, yet just as determined. They stopped about halfway down the corridor. Thomas placed his finger to his lips and raised his hand, signaling for stillness. They held their breath as she imagined the new person examining the drone.

"Who did this?" It was the voice of Lindzel.

"We are unable to ascertain the answer to your question your majesty." One of the guards spoke.

"Well bring up the footage, you idiot."

"There is no footage," the other guard piped in. "the cameras have been wiped."

*Cameras?* Alex whipped her head around to look at Thomas. He was staring at her, jaw set, pity in his eyes. *He saw.*

"I did no such thing." Lindzel was outraged. There was a burning sound and particles of metal dropped to the ground. Alex thought of the pile of robot dust from the throne room and suspected that two guards was now one.

"Find her." The command was cool and collected. "Kill her this time. We have no need for more rabble stirring up trouble." The lighter footsteps began walking away.

"And clean this place up. It's disgusting! And change the camera codes, lock them to anyone but me." She hollered back the afterthought as the door closed. Thomas and Alex stared at each other, waiting for the other guard to leave. After a few minutes, with no one left to guard, he turned and left the room.

"This way," Thomas began down the tunnel. His hand moved to his wrist and a beam of light sprang out lighting the way. The tunnel was long, too long for the light to penetrate. Alex followed him, her feet soaked through by the cold, filthy water. They walked in silence for a few moments, neither willing to bring up the topic that hung in the air.

"How did you find me?" Her voice barely a whisper, Alex broke the silence.

"I told you. I tracked you." His voice was cold and angry, which made Alex bitter in return. *Who was he to be angry? It's her life. She had the right to do with it as she pleased.*

"I heard you the first time." She spat back. "But *how* did you track me? Why wouldn't you have gone to the dungeons before now if you could *track* people so easily?" The last part of the sentence was biting, but she was tired of being judged.

"Your shirt, I placed a tracking bead on it, at your waist. I figured you'd be stupid enough to get caught." His words bit. He didn't look back. Alex looked down at the delicate beads she had admired so many times.

"You used me?!" she was suddenly outraged. "You knew I would be captured? The sweet innocent farm boy act really works for you. *Here, have some boots, have some food, you'll have to be careful.*" She attempted to mimic his voice but added a patronizing zing. She stopped and watched as he walked ahead of her. "You're just as bad as they are!" This time, the words seemed to hit home, since he stopped a few feet ahead. He didn't turn.

"You have no idea what you're talking about." The now knee-deep water splashed in every direction as he swirled around to look at her. His eyes were narrowed into tiny slits, and he looked like a viper ready to strike. "You show up here, stick your nose into business you know nothing about. People have been fighting the Queen for years. You've been in the dungeon; you've seen the stakes. She's *killing* people, *torturing* people, all for her own glory. She's erected a blight on the land that's going to wipe us all out if we don't stop her." He moved within inches of her. Spit flew from his mouth, and his harsh whisper grew louder with each word.

"Not to mention the hurt she has caused by ripping families apart. I knew there wasn't *much* chance, but there *was* a chance of finding them. I *had* to try. Do you understand that!? No matter how small the chance, I *had* to try! It's clear now. There is no hope. There's nothing left for me here. There's no reason for me to wait any longer. They're dead." He turned and abruptly continued walking.

Alex realized her selfishness instantly. Of course, Thomas had been trying to find a way into the castle for who knows how long. He had no way of knowing where the dungeon was. If she was captured, he could locate her, and he may have been able to locate his parents. It didn't make her less angry about him playing with her life so casually, but at least she understood why he had done it.

A sense of regret flooded over her, and she continued following in silence. Neither of them said anything for the rest of the way down the tunnel. Every so often, they walked under a city grate and heard a scuffle of guards rushing past. Each time they held their breath and waited for everyone to pass. The maze of tunnels was long and confusing. Just when she thought they were heading out of The Park, they turned a corner and headed back in. She couldn't tell if Thomas was just being cautious and doubling back, or if he was in fact lost.

Eventually, the water funneled through a large tub container. Its metallic green coating was a stark contrast to the dark stones that surrounded it. The liquid entered one side and every few minutes, out the other side, came a compacted brown dehydrated disc. Alex didn't have to imagine what it was made of. It was pushed out into an opening about half the size of the tunnel where they currently resided and disappeared downward. Thomas motioned with his head.

"Jump."

"What?! I'm not jumping down there. Where does it go? How far…"

He shrugged and jumped, disappearing down the hole before she had a chance to finish her sentence. Uncertain, she followed.

# CROSSROAD

Alex landed with a thud on a pile of brown discs. The tube extended at a forty-five-degree angle from the wall, adjacent to a set of similar tubes. The piles were almost high enough to reach the bottom of the tubes themselves, so the fall had been short once she entered the open air. There were large, square, unmanned machines gathering up material from the piles and compacting them into smaller masses of raw material. To her left, a pile of scrap metal discs was sorted into type and melted inside the machine before coming back out as what she assumed were usable bars. It was ingenious, and Alex couldn't help but wonder how there seemed to be so much pollution around them if there was such care paid to the reuse of materials.

With all the piles of reusable materials and compost discs, there was an equally disturbing amount of unusable waste. Piles of screens, odd looking devices and wires spanned for kilometers. Some of the piles were higher than the city walls. This must have been the Wasteland Thomas had collected most of his material from. For every broken item, there appeared to be an almost new one. Not all of it was boxy and undefined. The artistic energy put into the creation of most of the items was astounding. A pile of synthetic trees lay just to her left, as far as she could tell from her current position, each branch and leaf had been designed with care and precision. If she hadn't seen the fake vegetation in The Park earlier, she would have been outraged at the stack of perfectly good trees just torn out of the ground and cast aside.

Thomas was already at the bottom of the pile, and Alex

scrambled to catch up. A smoky haze filled the air, choking her breath as she ran toward her retreating savior. The source of the smoke was a burning pit on the other side of the Wasteland. Another large compactor was pushing piles of clothing and other textiles into the pit. Apparently, they didn't believe in reusing, or sharing, their clothing. If something could be reused for their own purposes, the "Parkians" seemed to be okay with that, but if it meant benefiting anyone in the lower city, then reuse was off limits. Thomas slowed as he reached the edge of the landfill. Several guards patrolled the perimeter. He ducked behind a pile of cone-shaped plastic gizmos of varying bright colours. Alex tucked in behind him.

"Look," she whispered, "I'm sorry. I didn't think. I forgot about..."

He raised his hand to silence her. They waited as the two guards passed each other on their rounds. When their backs were visible and they were far enough away, Thomas half jogged toward the edge of the garbage sea. Alex matched his crouching position and pace, resigned to wait until they were clear of danger before trying to get any more out of him. How could she have been so stupid? If it had been her parents locked away, she too would have done anything to get them out. She knew what it was like to find out your parent was gone, dead, never coming back. To lose both in one day would be unbearable. Alex's heart panged as she thought of her mother. She wondered what was happening to her at that moment.

Once they were clear of the dump, Thomas slowed his pace and ducked into the shadows. Safely on the streets of the lower city, he relaxed slightly but continued his determined gait. He didn't look around once to check if she was following. Judging by the direction of the wall, she guessed they were heading back toward the market district and his home. However, as they got closer, he turned and headed in the opposite direction.

Alex ran up to him and touched his shoulder. "Thomas?" He shook her off. "Thomas please!" Her voice cracked as she pleaded. Her desperation finally made him soften and he at least stopped. They were almost out of the city. He said nothing; he just stared at her, detached, waiting for her to speak.

"You're right, I don't have any idea what you've been through. I don't know how bad it has been for you, but you *must* understand that I know how you feel." She paused and an image of her father, smiling at her as she came home from school, flashed in her head. "I lost my dad about a year ago. Honestly, that's when I started giving up. Things got bad, really bad, for me. Yes, they were bad in different ways, but bad just the same."

Alex shuffled on her feet, she had been hoping to avoid the topic altogether, but she felt she owed her liberator an explanation. She continued. "Back there... I was just... I didn't know that you were coming... I just...." Tears began to stream down her face once again as she tried desperately to explain the anguish that was going on in her heart. There was no way that she could think of articulating how badly she wanted everything to be over, but seeing Thomas persevere through so much, beat the odds, gave her hope. At the very least, it showed her that his hope had been created through perseverance.

What came next, as she had found out the hard way, would determine who he became. She hoped, for him, that this loss would do more for him than it did for her. She felt a hand on her shoulder; it was warmer than she expected, and he pulled her in, hugging her. They embraced, feeling each other's pain, and sharing each other's strength for a long moment. It was the first time she'd felt at peace since the accident.

"Where will you go next? What will you do?" she prodded. The hint of a smile crept across his face.

"Well, I suppose the only thing left is to join the rebellion. I'm off to find Oothro." Thomas smiled expectantly. Alex rolled her eyes. It was obvious now that it had been his plan the whole time to help her escape and find the resistance. She wasn't sure what he would have done if his parents had still been alive, but he seemed a little more excited than he ought to be about his new path.

"When do we leave?"

"Now." He smiled and walked down the road leading out of the city.

# RENEWABLE

As they walked, Alex and her companion reached a bridge under the main highway. "This road leads to The Park," Thomas said. "But anyone coming from the highway would have a long walk ahead of them." They passed under the bridge and the forest beyond came into view. The trees were vast, but a huge barren waste lay in the distance eating away at the North part of the forest. The landscape stretched out before them, barren and desolate. The ground was scorched and blackened, cracked and broken by the intense heat of the concentrated solar radiation. Not a single blade of grass or tree stood tall, only the occasional twisted and withered remains of a shrub or cactus dotted the desolate terrain. As they got closer, the air was thick with the stench of burnt earth and ash. In the distance, the large circular monuments shimmered with a hazy, wavering heat that distorted the view. It was an eerie and silent wasteland that seemed to go on forever, as if time itself had stopped there.

"The cause of the decay is to the North," Thomas said. "The rings are hundreds of stories high. The energy field inside concentrates the solar radiation." They watched as a bird flew into the waste and collapsed into ash. "We need to be careful," he warned.

"What happened here?" Alex breathed.

"Do you remember the *great* power source I told you about the night we first met? Here you have it, the answer to all our problems." He motioned with sarcastic disappointment toward the barren waste. "It was once the greatest achievement of our time, and it might have stayed that way if people hadn't been so greedy.

Everyone, including those in the lower city, was ecstatic when it was proposed and erected. Many volunteered their time to work on the project for the promises that it held. The rings generate the city's power. I told you that they draw their power from the sun. It was an amazing discovery, a renewable energy source, available for all. Of course, the people in The Park area had always been richer than the rest of us, but even they couldn't deny the usefulness of such a great invention. It came at a time when the Queen was first losing favour with her court. Whispers of desertion were spreading across the lower city, and she was naturally ecstatic to have a reason to avoid mutiny. That was before the walls, before the split in the city, and before everything went terribly wrong."

He found a spot on the ground and they sat. The grass beneath them was soft, and, best of all, natural. Alex ran her hand through it as she listened. "What I didn't tell you is that the more energy that was required, the hotter and more radiant the rings became. At first, there was only one ring, but the more technologies people invented, the more power that was required. The Queen's first answer was to restrict technology use in the lower city. The division between rich and poor became even more defined when this happened."

"But it doesn't make sense." Alex picked at a blade of grass. Thomas pulled out a small bun and handed it to her. She gladly accepted it and finished the rest of her question with her mouth full, "Why din't day stop inbenting sings?"

Thomas smiled at her slightly before continuing his story, a twinkle in his eye indicating that he was more than simply amused by her bun filled question. "It didn't take long before the Queen didn't need people to invent anymore. One of the local toy makers had created a robot. You've likely seen copies of him in the castle. His name was Rab, and he was unbelievably loyal to his father and his family. The Queen, however, wanted the android's loyalty for herself. She tortured the poor man relentlessly, so the stories go, until he agreed to transfer the programming to her. The Queen had a robot slave that was smarter than any human she could even enslave.

"They didn't seem all that smart to me." Alex interjected.

"I'll get to that." He continued, "The inventions continued to get more complex, and the people in The Park rejoiced with each new entertainment. Soon, things ceased to have practical applications, and at the direction of the Queen, more was created that would delight her and her strong cult following."

Thomas stared out into the barren waste. "We should move."

"What do you mean? Why? What happened after that?" She sounded like a toddler at bedtime, wishing the story to continue.

"We've been lucky so far," Thomas cautioned, "but the drones will be out soon. The sun is disappearing. We should get some distance between us and the city before finding a spot to camp for the night." He stood and turned to help her up, but she was already standing by the time he looked. His shoulders fell, looking a bit disappointed that she didn't need his help. Alex, however, had no desire to meet the drones in a combat situation and was eager to get moving.

Thomas pulled out the tablet that Alex had been given before her capture. Apparently, he had liberated more than her. They consulted the map and started out. As they left the rings behind, the forest became denser and greener. As they ventured further into the forest, the air grew cooler and the light dimmer. The crunch of twigs and leaves underfoot softened as the ground became covered in a thick carpet of moss. The trees grew taller and closer together, creating a canopy that blocked out most of the sun. As their eyes adjusted to the dimness, they noticed that the greenery around them grew more abundant and vibrant. Delicate ferns sprouted from fallen logs, while vibrant wildflowers peppered the ground. The foliage became so dense that they had to push through overhanging branches to continue forward. Sunbeams filtered through the canopy, casting a dappled light on everything below. It was as if they had entered another world, a verdant paradise hidden within the depths of the forest.

Alex had allowed the serene surroundings to lull her into a false sense of calmness, when Thomas's grip tightened around her arm and yanked her down a steep embankment without warning. He pushed her up and under a hollow decaying log as he held his hand over her mouth. Her heart raced as she listened for whatever it was that had distressed him. Now that she was listening, she could hear the mechanical sound of tracks rolling along the ground. Judging by the fast acceleration of sound, it was a vehicle of some kind, and the loud snapping of logs meant that it was large!

"Sentinel." He whispered; his lips so close to her ears they were almost touching.

When Thomas was satisfied that they were hidden and that Alex wasn't going to scream out, he let go of her. The blood rushed back into her arm where he had been gripping tightly and she rubbed the spot where a bruise was sure to form.

"Sorry." He apologized and looked away and focused his attention on peeking up over the ledge. Alex slid in beside him, still rubbing her arm.

The sun had almost disappeared behind the horizon, and the twilight made it difficult to see all the details of the giant vehicle that approached. However, what she could make out was shocking. It looked like an enormous humanoid robot, only instead of moving along with jointed legs and arms, the contraption rolled along on tank-like treads. Its arms swiveled with full range of motion in every direction, casting a beam of light on the ground wherever it faced. The beam swept the ground in front of them and Thomas pulled Alex back down the embankment.

"Owww!" she squawked. He had pulled her by grabbing the same spot he had previously. At this point, the noise from the Sentinel was louder than any complaint she could muster, so Thomas didn't make any motion to cover her mouth again, but he did give her another apologetic look. Once the beam had passed, they were back up at their post.

The enormous treads crushed everything in their path. Even huge trees, still standing, were no match for the Sentinel. Several guns mounted on the sentinel's legs and arms swiveled in every direction. Atop the goliath's shoulders sat a round domed head. The entire dome was transparent and showed two actual humans sitting at a control panel. Obviously, the Queen hadn't managed to place AI in all her creations. Not seeing anything of interest, the patrol continued past them toward the city.

"Well," Thomas half whispered, "I suppose this is as good a place to rest as any." She helped gather branches with as many leaves left as possible and they leaned them against their temporary hiding place to make a shelter for the evening. Thomas took off his outer tunic and handed it to Alex, who was shivering.

"We can't start a fire. It will draw too much attention."

Alex nodded and scanned the makeshift shelter cautiously before entering. She recalled the eight-legged monster that had accosted her when she first arrived in Wonderland. Sleeping in the forest without a sealed tent didn't really appeal to her. However, her body felt heavy with the events of the day, and she eventually tucked herself as far into the temporary shelter as possible. She wasn't tired. Too much had happened today for her to quiet her mind enough to sleep.

"So," she spoke as he finished making himself comfortable. "You were saying that there was only one of these *Rabs*. I saw three of them when I was in the castle. Where did they come from?"

Thomas nodded, remembering where he had left off. "That's just it," he continued. "One was never enough for the Queen. She thought that if she could have more robots like Rab, that things would prosper and grow even faster. Rab, however, was only able to duplicate the very basic functions that he performed. It was his father that created his intelligence. He was unable to duplicate it. The new 'Rabs' never had any intelligence of their own. All they could do was mimic the original's mannerisms.

"Nevertheless, progress continued. The walls went up, making the power requirements unattainable with only one ring. As you saw, two more power rings were erected, this time using mechanical power. The thousands of white robots worked day and night until they were completed. When one broke down, they were tossed in the garbage pile, and another was made. Once the third ring was in place, the land began to die at an exponential rate."

"That's what I don't get," Alex shook her head and frowned. "How does solar energy ruin the environment? It's supposed to be better than other forms of energy, isn't it?"

"If the single ring had been left on its own, it likely would have continued to thrive for many years. You see, the rings use very focused mirrors to direct the sun's energy into two single points in the middle of the smaller rings. From there, the energy is directed at a field that disperses the heat and recycles it continually until it can be converted by the larger ring into the energy needed for the grid." Thomas' eyes seemed to brighten as he talked about the mechanics of the technology. She recognized the look as the one her father had when he explained some new scientific breakthrough over the dinner table. Even though he was frustrated by the outcome of the technology, he seemed to appreciate the ingenuity in its creation. His face, however, turned grave as he continued. "The longer the ring is active, the more focused the energy becomes. If the energy meters are turned up to full, the radiation that gets through the atmosphere is gathered along with the sun's heat, this makes the energy field very dangerous."

Alex shivered. The tunic that Thomas had lent her was helping, but the chill in the air was more than she had anticipated once the sun went down. Seeing her discomfort, Thomas moved over and placed his arm around her. Alex stiffened, unsure what to do with this new sensation.

"The worst part is the build up of radiation that comes from the increase in power storage. Not only was the ground being burnt, but traces of the sun's radiation were also being transferred to the land. It's poison to anyone who touches it. Remember the bird?" Alex hadn't thought about it since, but she nodded her acknowledgment.

"We should get some sleep. It's going to be a long walk tomorrow." Alex felt her exhaustion creep in, built from several days of running. She wasn't sure how long she had been in Wonderland, but it felt like weeks had passed by already. She leaned her head against Thomas' chest and listened to his breathing; it was the most comfortable and safe she had ever remembered feeling.

# EASY?

Her eyes fluttered open to the sound of rustling, and leaves fell into her mouth. She spit them out as Thomas deconstructed the shelter they had made the night before.

"We can't leave any trace. They'll be looking for us, or you rather." He scattered the last of the branches and examined her filth-stained pack from the day before. Most of its contents were useless, and the food wasn't any good, but he pulled out the bedroll and cloak that had been too damp the night before. They were dry now, but crunchy in spots.

"I think we need to get a few more supplies before venturing into the forest. It's only a few days, but I don't think we should spend another night like last night, as comfortable as I was." He winked at her, and Alex noticed a white drool stain on his tunic where she had rested her head. She was mortified, but he said nothing else about it.

They ducked in and out of the trees as they scanned the perimeter of the forest for signs of life. While most of the patrols used mechanical robots and androids, there was always the need for technicians, and computer engineers to keep things running smoothly. Thomas predicted that there would be a camp nearby, and after twenty minutes of searching, they found their prize.

They skulked around the perimeter counting their opposition and making predictions about which machines were dormant, down for repair or active. Luckily, most of the patrols were already out for the day. The beauty of using machines was that there was very little need for them to return to the camp unless they needed some care. As luck would have it, this was good for Alex and Thomas too. Without the machines to contend with, it would be a basic stealth in and stealth out affair.

Alex followed Thomas. A few times she caught herself admiring how his body moved under his tunic but quickly pushed those thoughts aside, scolding herself. He snuck around the perimeter of the camp like a professional thief. He must be used to avoiding the guards while sneaking his items from the dump, but his skill bordered on criminal. She averted her eyes, pretending that she was watching for danger each time he looked back at her, but she suspected she was fooling no one.

The far tent seemed the most promising. Barrels and crates were stacked outside, and people dressed in civilian clothing busied themselves stacking, unpacking, and counting the new shipments. There were blankets, outer cloaks, and rations for the entire camp. To get there, they had to either go around the perimeter of the camp, forcing them across the main road, or go straight through, using building for cover. The main road was constantly in use. Carts showed up with parts, and the guard stationed at the entrance checked items on a clipboard as each entered. When he wasn't busy with carts, he was pacing back and forth across the road, watching for movement in the trees and pathways. There were opportunities to make a break when everyone was distracted with a shipment, but there would be more eyes to avoid. Not that the other option didn't have its own risks.

The camp was filled with tents, wagons, robots, and cooking fires. It looked as if the men in the camp had set up their homes and had been here for quite some time already. Periodically she spotted someone that didn't quite seem to fit in. A subtle head shake, a heavy sigh as they observed their surroundings. Clearly not everyone was satisfied with their position and task. Yet, judging by the comfortable setup of their belongings, they also seemed thankful that they weren't stuck in the Cistern.

Not all the men and women in the camp seemed complacent with their positions. In fact, there were just as many who seemed to revel in their power, looking down on those that showed less pride or pushing around their subordinates. *It's like being at school all over again* she thought.

Her mind wandered momentarily as she recalled the churning sea of students hunched over food trays and lined up at tables in groups like chattering chipmunks. If they chose to go through the camp, they would have more hiding spots, and more people to avoid. It was a tough decision. She turned to Thomas, more familiar with Wonderland stealth missions. He seemed eager to take the direct route.

"Um, perhaps I should just wait here," Alex whispered from the shadows. She was doubting her ability and her bravery. "Besides, I'm sure we can do without food for a few days."

"The rotations follow a pattern," he said reassuringly, "so we can predict how to stay hidden. It's impossible for me to carry everything and remain undetected. That's where I need you." There was an underlying meaning in his voice that suggested she was more than a pack mule, and he waited for her confirmation before dashing off towards a wagon positioned between two tents. Once he was safely concealed, he turned to check on her progress. While she was used to skulking in the shadows, mission impossible style covert operations. She hadn't moved. Fear paralyzed her.

Another flash brought a lump to her throat as she recalled the journey she took daily, dodging between groups of pressed and labeled students as she moved from one class to the next. Snippets of conversation met her ears as she counted the steps to her destination. It wouldn't be the first time she had to duck into an alcove unnoticed. *He's right. I got this!* She tried to pump herself up.

An idea sparked, and she scanned the camp. A few young girls traveled with trays from tent to tent, bringing the afternoon meal to the people still working on various tasks. Used trays were left Infront of tents for pickup. One thing that running from bullies had taught her was to blend into a crowd. She wasn't good at crouching and ducking and jumping, but she *could* be invisible.

Her eyes locked with Thomas' asking for some trust. Instead of running and skidding into hiding, she waited until no one was watching and casually walked into the camp. Picking up a tray from the nearest tent, she hung her head, refusing to make eye contact, and walked back toward the large supply tent. No one looked up. She didn't dare look around to see if Thomas was following her, but she trusted that he too knew what he needed to do. Upon arriving, she placed the tray in the pile that was forming and sauntered into the supply tent.

*Shit. Shit. Shit. Now what?* She cursed to herself as she moved to a shelf and began folding blankets. From the back wall she heard Thomas' whisper through the heavy cloth.

"You're brilliant!" he whispered, "bloody crazy, but brilliant!"

"Ya right," she whispered back, "I'm so smart I've trapped myself." One of the other girls walked by with a crate full of PCDs, giving Alex a questioning sidelong look. Alex smiled and pulled a crate of potatoes off the shelf and nodded at the girl. Apparently, they didn't have food replicators in the work camps. The girl walked away, eyeing Alex the whole time. Once she was out of earshot Alex continued. "If I don't get out of here soon, I don't think my bright idea will pan out so well," she hissed.

"Pass some stuff under." His voice was urgent but kind.

She worked as quickly as she could, shoving a few blankets, some rope, a couple of cloaks, and some rations that would last a few days under the flap at the back of the tent. The tent was on the very edge of the camp, so she presumed and hoped that Thomas was safe enough on the other side. When he indicated that they had collected enough, she walked out of the tent as quickly as she could while remaining casual.

As she rounded the tent, the young girl she had encountered earlier was talking to an older adult and pointing at Alex. Panic consumed her, and she darted past the tent, searching for Thomas and the supplies. Thomas was nowhere in sight, and Alex didn't know where to go next. The camp was alerted of an intruder, and she could hear the robot patrollers powering up. Running toward the trees, she closed her eyes and ran like she'd never run before. The only thing on her mind was Mr. Stuckey, her gym teacher, and how proud he would be of her efforts. Apparently, she had it in her, she just had to be chased by vaporizing robot sentinels to prove it.

The sounds of the camp, the guards, and the commotion began to fade away, but she couldn't bring herself to stop. She continued to run until there were no sounds left in the forest but those of the birds. The entire time, she thought of Tasha, her gang, every teacher that had criticized her, and her father's coffin being lowered into the grave. Her body told her to stop, but her mind told her to run, just keep running and perhaps she would get far enough away that the haunting images in her head would disappear with her pursuers.

All at once, she was wrapped in a grey woolen sheath that stopped her dead in her tracks. The force of her running combined with the sudden stop knocked the wind out of her. She panicked, punching outward at her attacker, trying desperately to see what had confined her. The force of it constricted her. She flailed, but it was no use. The being holding her steady was gripping her tighter as she struggled to get away. The woolen fabric that was wrapped around her made it impossible for her to see what was around her.

"Shhhhh," she heard over her own screams. "Alex, it's me." The voice was a pleading whisper. Somehow, Thomas had run ahead and now decided it was time to stop her. Knowing she was finally safe, she melted into his arms, crumbling to her knees and pulling the blanket around her. The once constricting blanket became a cocoon of comfort. She panted, trying desperately to catch her breath, but her body was feeling every bit how out of shape she actually was.

# EASIER?

Once Alex had calmed down enough to take in her surroundings, she noticed that the trees in this part of the forest were much fuller. The green leaves were almost shining in comparison with the barren charred edges of the forest. Thomas let her catch her breath while he fashioned a pack out of the rope and blanket. Seeing his handiwork, Alex tried to mimic the actions and make a pack of her own. It certainly wasn't as beautiful, but it held her portion of the supplies.

According to the map, there would be at least another day and a half walk before they reached the cave. She wasn't sure where Thomas would go to join the rebellion, but they both assumed that Oothro would be the key to all their questions.

Deeper into the forest the threat from city forces was still present, but much less oppressive. More than a few times Thomas and Alex ducked into the underbrush to avoid detection, but for the time being, without the threat of imminent death, they were able to relax.

"How long has your father been gone?" Thomas cut the silence that had settled around them. The question made Alex uncomfortable, and she fidgeted with the buttons on her shirt.

"A little over a year." She continued walking, making an effort to avoid eye contact. Another silence enveloped them, this time a note of awkwardness in the air.

After about ten seconds Thomas broke in again. "All this time I thought I could save them, that they'd been waiting for me to save them. I had... hope." His voice cracked. "Does it get easier?" This time the silence that followed was even longer. Eventually, Alex turned to look at him and was surprised by the silent tears streaming down his face. She searched her memory for something to say, something to comfort him as he silently sobbed beside her. None of the advice spouted at her after her father passed seemed adequate. The hollow words hadn't comforted her at the time, and there was little chance that they would hit their mark this time. Flashes of her own grief clouded her memory as she stumbled over to find the words to say.

Thomas spoke again, as if he sensed he was making her uncomfortable. "It's okay. I didn't mean to make you uncomfortable. I'm sorry." He wiped away his tears and stood up straighter, taking a deep breath in and tilting his chin up slightly. Seeing the familiar stance she once took when pushing down her feelings, the mental block lowered.

"No. I can't tell you what will make you feel better, but I can tell you what is real. You will get angry. You will get so angry that you start blaming everyone for everything, even those trying to help you. It's okay to be angry."

"Thank you," his voice registered closure on the subject but Alex continued.

"Triggers will be everywhere. You *will* be reminded of them, and you *will* have sudden awkward outbursts because of it. No one will know how to deal with you, so they'll say nothing, or say something stupid. They'll compare your grief with losing a pet or losing a close friend. They'll tell you everything will be alright, that you'll get back to normal soon enough. They'll tell you it's okay to cry, that you should let it all out and you'll feel better. It doesn't make you feel better. The more they try to help, the more you'll hate them, and push them away. The more they push, the more you'll pretend everything is fine, so they'll just leave you alone. You'll want to yell at them; to punch them. When they finally do leave you alone because they think you're fine, you'll feel abandoned, alone, and confused. Time does *not* heal all wounds." Once she started, she couldn't stop. Outlining all the absurd things she had experienced over the past year was oddly therapeutic. Thomas saw that he couldn't close the floodgate, and let her continue.

"You can plan for death, even your own, but death does not always comply with our wishes or plans." At this she stopped walking and looked him in the eyes. She knew he had seen her back in the cell. She acknowledged this with a glance, and he nodded back his understanding. "It is normal to feel numb. The tears will come.

They come in waves. It is okay not to cry. You will never go back to being your "old self". Grief changes you, and you are never the same. You'll never get over it, but you will get used to it. Nothing you do in the future will change your love for them, but eventually, you will begin to enjoy life again." She reached out and grabbed his hand, "And you may even meet someone that makes it feel better. Remember, whatever you find to bring you joy won't diminish your love for them."

Her sentences were becoming disjointed and list-like as if she was going through everything that had once been said to her and was disputing it. Many of the words she was hearing and thinking for the first time herself, the sudden epiphany coming in the form of helping someone else. It felt as if she was a bystander listening to her own sermon. For the first time, she was seeing how her own life had unfolded after her father's passing. She saw how she had closed herself off from the one person that understood what she was going through, and unexpectedly missed her mother more at this moment than she had since arriving. She could see now that her mother had needed her too, yet she had closed her bedroom door, closed her life, and closed her heart to everyone.

Thomas placed a comforting arm around her and pulled her in. His lips were centimeters from her forehead, and she almost wished he would just kiss the top of her head and pull her in for a tight embrace.

"Thank you." This time, his voice was less absolute and more sincere. He wasn't just trying to end the conversation; he was acknowledging an end to the deeply felt waves of grief that had been plaguing his new friend for many months. Judging by the stiffness in his body, his own wounds were still too raw to find closure, but somehow Alex could tell by his touch that he was on the right path to recovery. She placed her arm around his waist in a similar show of support before they continued their walk through the thickening forest.

As the night fell, their conversation turned more casual. They talked about what Alex did for fun in her world, and Thomas was fascinated by the concept of schools where thousands of children went to learn about the world every day. Alex chuckled at the thought of someone wishing they could go to school. When it seemed like the night was almost upon them, they stopped to make a shelter, this time starting a small fire for warmth. It was still important for them to set up a patrol. Thomas took the first watch.

# THIS ISN'T…

When Thomas shook her awake, it was dark. The night air was cold on her cheeks, but the blankets they 'borrowed' from the camp provided her with insulated heat. She didn't want to leave its warm embrace, but Thomas looked dreadful. His eyes were swollen and red, and she knew that he'd been crying most of the night. The fire had calmed to a pile of embers. Thomas placed a small piece of a log on it and indicated that they should keep it low to avoid detection. He silently curled up in the already warm pile of blankets and drifted off to sleep.

Alex didn't know what to do to pass the time. She had no desire to be left alone with her thoughts and she fidgeted with her hands as she scanned the seemingly empty forest. She walked out of the camp as far as the light allowed, searching for anything interesting to occupy her time. The plants in this part of the forest were different than those she was used to seeing back home. The trees still looked basic enough, but their bark formed a crisscross pattern instead of the traditional up and down bumpy texture she was used to. She ran her hands up and down the trunks and noticed that the plaid pattern was perfectly spaced along the smooth surfaces. The leaves were also unusual. The underside of these leaves were luminescent. They let off a faint light that lit the ground below, allowing Alex to see shadows well beyond the edge of their camp. As she reached the outer edge of the firelight, she noticed a brighter glow just beyond her view. Alex assumed that Thomas must have seen it too, since it seemed to stay unmoving. He hadn't alerted her to any danger, so she figured checking it out was as good a distraction as any.

Walking through the trees, she heard the scurrying of small animals as they rushed for cover to avoid the invading giant. She shivered to think of what may be scuttling in the dark, but steeled her resolve and pushed the thought out of her mind as childish worry. The closer she got to the light, the clearer the source became. A grouping of bushes bore thousands of tiny lights. It looked as if someone had decorated it for Christmas and forgotten to take the lights down once the season ended. As she got closer, she could see that the lights weren't bulbs at all. Instead, thousands of brightly lit berries illuminated the night. They looked like glowing blueberries. As she examined it closer, a faint hum emanated from them and she could tell it was one of the trees they had eaten berries off of earlier that day. Thomas hadn't mentioned that the berries glowed at night! She would have to scold him in the morning for leaving out such a fascinating detail.

Remembering the sweet burst of juice from earlier, Alex's mouth watered. As she plucked a berry off the tree, it lost its luster and glow, and she delighted in the novelty. She picked a handful, careful not to crush them, and breathed in their scent. The freshness of them was intoxicating and only made her want to devour them even more. Tipping her head back she popped them all in her mouth at once. They were divine. The sweetness was even more prominent this evening than it had been earlier that day. She wondered if it had something to do with the glow.

A few seconds later the world began to wobble and spin. This hadn't happened earlier that day. A numbness spread across her tongue. Spinning around, trying to orientate herself she noticed the light from the camp appeared closer and further away at the same time. The bushes in front of her moved back and forth, looking as if they were meters away for one second, then right beside her in another second. She became dizzy and her head spun, and she lowered herself to the ground for stability. She closed her eyes and waited for the moment to pass.

# IT'S TIME

The light around her was as bright as midday when Alex opened her eyes even though it only seemed like a matter of seconds since she had closed them. Instead of Wonderland and Thomas she was surrounded by the familiar scene of a hospital room. She shook her head a few times, trying to figure out where she was and why she was in the hospital. She was confused and disoriented.

Her mother sat across the room, book in hand. *Is that my journal?* She seemed much older and worn than Alex remembered. Alex wasn't sure anymore which world was real, perhaps they both were. She had only been in the hospital room for a few minutes, yet in Wonderland, the entire night had flown by.

"Mom?" she croaked. "what's going…"

Her mother looked up, cutting her off, "Alex!" the journal she was reading dropped to the floor without a second thought and she bolted toward her daughter.

"Alex, stay with us this time."

"Mom? What…" a sharp pain pressed into her temples. She instinctively grabbed her head and squinted her eyes shut. Behind her eyes a bright white light felt as if it was going to blind her.

The smell of moss and earth came back to her. When she opened her eyes this time, Thomas hunched over her. Every so often as his head moved and the sun, which was now overhead, shone directly in her eyes. She squinted,

"Thank God!" He wrapped his arms around her, lifting her partially from her laying position. She surprised herself by returning the embrace. "I found you in the forest. I've been trying to wake you all day! You've been lying her for hours. I was afraid to move you. What happ-."

"Thomas!" She was surprised to find that she was happy to see him, more than happy. Her arms flung around him tightly. She hadn't realized how fond she had grown of him until she had been pulled so abruptly away. In return, he wrinkled in confusion. The bush full of berries from the night before sat inconspicuously beside them. The fruit had lost its glow, and they looked like extremely unexceptional berries.

"Hungry?" Thomas followed her gaze to the patch of bushes, plucking a few off its branches.

"No!" she protested. His eyes widened at her adverse reaction.

"Alright," he chuckled. "I thought you liked them yesterday." The handful of fruit tumbled into his mouth. Alex's heart leaped. Nothing happened.

"You sure?" he offered again, but she just shook her head, confused. The packs had already been secured and each was leaning against a rock close by.

"Let's get going." She suggested and laboured to stand as she worked out the stiffness that had set in from laying on the ground for hours. The pack seemed heavier today.

It was midday by the time she had risen, but their travel was more relaxed. They assumed there would be no reason for the guard to patrol this deeply into the forest. It was likely the reason Oothro decided to live so deep into Wonderland's expanse of trees. Without the deadly radiation from the rings, the forest was thriving. In the daylight, Alex could get a much better view of the different varieties of plants and flowers she had examined the night before. Everything seemed oversized, like it was built for giants. They passed flowers with blossoms the size of full-grown adults and the trees were so tall that she couldn't see the tops of them. Their trunks were so thick that Alex was sure it would take fifteen people just to wrap their arms around them. The colours of the forest were equally impressive and vibrant. Bright purple leaves sprang from some of the bushes. Fluorescent pink, yellow, and green flowers matched the highlighters in her pencil case back home. Even the trunks of the trees had an orange hue to them.

It was early evening when they came across a rundown old cottage. Looking at the tablet she noticed it wasn't on the map, so the sight surprised them both. There were holes in the roof, and the grass had overgrown the stone fence that surrounded the property. By all indications, no one had lived there for years. They approached with caution. While it was clear that the home was unfit for human habitation, there was no guarantee about animal inhabitants. *Have we missed Oothro already?* Alex thought. Perhaps the baker had been sending people out here for years without even knowing that the hermit had moved on.

Listening carefully, they split up and looked through the windows. The glass was long gone, most of it broken and lying on the ground. Inside, the scene mirrored the long-forgotten feel of the exterior. Dust covered everything in a thick blanket. It was a single room cottage with a fireplace, bed, and a few cupboards and shelves. The cupboards had been emptied and the bed stripped indicating that the previous owners had moved out instead of fled. However, the most peculiar scene lay on the table in the center of the room. A perfectly laid out tea party with four places sat ready for guests. Each teacup was perfectly aligned with the next. A large teapot in the center of the table was big enough to hold tea for twenty. Two plates, empty, lay on either side of the pot. Alex imagined they'd once held delightful squares and tea cookies. She could see Thomas through the house, looking into the window on the other side of the single room. He nodded to her, suggesting that he felt it was safe. She returned with a nod of agreement and they made their way back to the front of the house where they met in front of the wooden door.

It was clean and was the only part of the house that looked relatively untouched by age. The handle on the door still gleamed brightly in the late afternoon sun. Thomas looked at her questioningly for a few seconds and then turned the handle and pushed his way into the house. Upon entering, they both stopped in their tracks. Instead of the dust-covered floor, inside lay a perfectly preserved home. The layout was identical to the one they had observed through the window, only everything in the room was clean and fresh. The panes of glass were clear and whole. Stunned, they simultaneously and wordlessly stepped back outside, parting ways, and returning to the windows they had peered in moments earlier. The view from the window was the same as they had previously witnessed, yet when they walked back to the doorway, the scene was quite different. Warily they entered the house once again. The bed was covered with a colourful and cozy looking quilt, and the hearth held a cozy fire. Bookshelves were overflowing with books and odd-looking gadgets. The table was still set for tea, only, this time, the plates were filled with delectable scones and cookies. A swirl of steam rose from the spout of the teapot. Either someone had just left, or they would be back soon.

Thomas moved into the room and began inspecting some of the books. Alex was drawn to the table set for tea. Beside the plate of treats lay a small note. Scrawled across it were the words, "Eat me," as if the owner of the house had been expecting guests. Perhaps he had set the house up to welcome weary travelers. Maybe it was Oothro's house? Either way, her curiosity got the better of her. Saliva pooled in her mouth as she scanned the plate of goodies. The food in this world, while a little unorthodox, had been delicious. While some of it had unexpected effects, nothing had ever harmed her, and in the end, had always led her toward a new goal and new experience. *Right?* She reasoned with herself. After a few moments of rationalization, she settled on a cake with powdery green icing.

The instant she took a bite, all her pores began to shrink. The room grew around her, or rather she shrunk. In an instant, she was on the ground. The cup she'd been holding lay broken next to her tiny body. The sound of the glass breaking caught Thomas' attention, and she saw the look of panic and frustration spread like a wave across his eyes.

"Nine Hells!" Thomas exclaimed.

The sound of his feet hitting the floor thundered through the room as he approached. The ground shook, and she scrambled to the leg of the table to stabilize herself. Thomas started by inspecting the food and plates on the table. He could clearly see that one was missing, and he opened the teapot to see what was inside. As the lid lifted from the pot, Alex heard a shifting and scraping noise coming from near the hearth. The noise would have been too small for Thomas to hear, but in her miniaturized state, everything was amplified. Something, perhaps the removal of the lid from the pot, seemed to have triggered a latch, and a tiny door, large enough for someone of her size opened next to the warm stones.

Alex moved behind the table leg, waiting for a hungry and angry beast to pounce out of the opening and possibly eat her. Instead, a small room appeared to lie beyond the door. Nothing exited. Thomas continued to walk about the room, looking for signs of her. She tried to call him, but her tiny cries were no match for the ambient noises in the room. Even the fire seemed louder than she could scream. After a few minutes, Thomas walked toward the door and left the room.

"No! Thomas!" she pleaded as loudly as she could muster but he was already gone. Scanning the room, her eyes fell once again on the tiny opening. She scurried toward it, careful to stay out of sight and along the walls in case the anticipated beast actually did appear.

The room beyond the door was identical to the one she had just been in. A small fireplace, complete with fire, was on the far wall. The same bed, with the same colourful quilt, was cuddled into the corner. It was as if someone had created a tiny hide away inside their own home to escape to. What she wouldn't give to have something like this back home. As with the previous room, the smaller version was void of occupants. The one difference was a desk that sat against the left wall. Its dark wood was inlaid with lighter orange-hued wood. Each inlaid piece represented a different plant design. Beakers and burners were set up on the desk, and stacks of papers and notes surrounded them. Alex was certain that her science teacher wouldn't approve of the hazard. The sight of it, however, delighted her. On her many visits to work with her father, she was often allowed to pop over to the Chemistry department. Her father often told them that if she asked too many questions, they could just send her back, but they never did.

Someone had gone through a lot of trouble to hide this secret lab from prying eyes. Her fingers riffled through the papers, but she didn't recognize the sketches. Some were of plants she had never seen, in this world or her own. There were recipes for potions or foods to make you change size. Others had solutions to disguise you, or change your skin colour, though she wasn't sure why you would want to do that. From the few snippets she read of the notes scrawled across the papers, she could make out that some recipes were to cure maladies, others seemed to have a purpose beyond her grasping. She stopped at the picture of the bush she had encountered the night before. There was no recipe attached, but in small scrawl at the bottom of the image, barely visible without squinting, were the instructions, *harvest at night*. A journal on the far end of the table had a single letter engraved in swirling calligraphy upon its cover. H

The sound of giant footsteps interrupted her inspection. They were coming from the room she had just vacated. Quickly and cautiously her tiny legs carried her back to the small door and peered outside. She let out her breath when she saw it was Thomas. He was calling to her, shaking his head, looking confused. He plunked himself down into a comfy looking armchair and held his head in his hands. Alex cursed as she was reminded of her predicament. In this room, everything looked ordinary size. She had completely forgotten her diminished state. How was she going to get out of this?

"The table!" she yelled out to no one. Swiveling, she beelined to the table in the center of the room and scanned it for anything familiar. On the plate, next to the teapot, lay a pile of the growth cakes like the one that Ches had given her on her first day in Wonderland. Pocketing two, she bit down on the third. Nothing happened.

Frustrated, she threw the rest of the cake across the room toward the fire. As her gaze followed its path, she noticed a map hanging above the hearth. She hadn't noticed it in the other room. She moved closer to inspect it and saw that it was delicately woven and embroidered. The images and lines looked like the crudely drawn map she had seen on the tablet, only this one was a lot more detailed. She took the delicate tapestry off the wall and noticed a few holes eaten away by time. Instead of a parched waste where the power rings had been erected, there sat a beautiful, forested area. The path they had followed was also outlined on the map. The house they were in was along the path, but it was much closer to the cave than her map would have indicated.

She poked her finger through one of the holes and noticed that her finger was growing inside the gap. Surprised, she dropped the tapestry, and it fell with a whoosh of heat into the fire. The map, however, hadn't been shrinking at all. In fact, she was growing! The cake must have allowed a delayed reaction so whoever ate it had time to escape the tiny room. She grew faster than she would have liked as she darted for the door on the other side of the hidden sanctuary. By the time she passed the table, her head was already hitting the roof. Once at the door, she could barely squeeze her body through, forcing her to clamor onto her hands and knees. The effects of the cake were escalating, and she dove through the opening, landing on her stomach. By the time she hit the floor, she was back to her normal size. Her left foot, unfortunately, had not been lucky enough to clear the doorway, and she tugged at it hopelessly.

"Alex!?" Thomas' voice was shocked from the other side of the room. "Where did you come from?"

"Great question," she responded tugging at her foot. "but first, a little help here?"

Thomas strode over trying to stifle his amusement. They twisted and angled her foot until it finally slipped out of the tiny doorway. As soon as she was free, the doorway slammed shut and the edges of it disappeared in a flash of light. They felt the trim where the edges had been, but the surface was once again smooth.

"So... about that story?" Thomas asked with his one eyebrow cocked.

# ONLY LOGICAL...

After Alex had relayed her tale, they decided to stay in the cottage overnight. They ate their rations and avoided everything on the table entirely. Based on what little she had read in the notes from the study, the food could be laced with just about anything. Of course, part of her wanted to take a nibble of everything, just to see what it would do but she refrained. Her dreams were troubled, and she couldn't stop thinking about her experience with the glowing berries. Had she actually been transported back to her world? The pain and joy on her mother's face flashed across her dreams. The image of her journal, perched in her mother's hands mortified her. She had found Alex's darkest secrets, most of which she now regretted thinking.

Exhaustion still gripped her when she finally wiped the crust from her eyes. They set out early. Either the day went by fast, or the cave was much closer than they had originally thought. Within the hour, they were at the mouth of a large hollow in the side of a small cliff. They approached with caution. In every book Alex had read, a dark abandoned cave never led to anything good, but the cave had been well marked on the map. It must have been put there for a reason.

The carvings along the mouth of the cave resembled fires with tendrils of smoke rising and morphing into shapes as they rose along the rock. There were dragons, ships, and castles intermingled with spaceships, mysterious symbols, and alien looking creatures. The craftsmanship was remarkable. As they approached each carving it started to move. Each morphed and changed as if they were flames flickering up from a fire. Alex reached out, wondering if this too was some sort of projection, but her fingers touched the creases in the stones, and she ran her fingers up and down them. There was no explanation for them, but her father's voice filled her mind, *things that can't be explained are merely things that haven't yet been discovered.*

Deeper inside, however, left much more to be desired. It was filled with a blackness as thick as oil. The light from outside was swallowed by the inky darkness after a few meters. They tried what lights they had on their devices but found none of them worked inside the cave. Thomas was looking around, to find something to make a torch, but they had nothing to light it. Each of them placed a hand on the wall and inched forward blindly hoping that eventually there would be an opening to or end to the darkness.

After a about a hundred meters the sound of rocks under their feet seemed to echo, indicating that the cave was starting to grow larger. Unfortunately, the lights didn't flicker on as they had in the halls of the dungeon. An earthy smell permeated the cavern, and Alex swatted in front of her when a long stringy tendril that turned out to be the root of a tree brushed her face. It was musty and growing damp, and Alex could faintly smell moss. Just when she thought they had better turn back, she felt Thomas' hand on her shoulder.

"Look… up ahead," he whispered, yet she saw nothing but the same raven blackness that was there moments ago.

"What? There's nothing there." She turned back toward the cave entrance but could no longer see in the direction they had come.

"The light. Don't you see it?" Her frustration came through in her sigh as she whirled around hoping that humouring him would hurry him out of the cave. Instead of blackness, however, she saw an ornate wooden desk sitting in the middle of the cave. It was about ten meters ahead of them. A single table lamp cast light around it making the desk glow in the warm yellow light. A tome sat unopened in the middle of it. The light flickered, as if dying, giving the scene a strobe effect. The book seemed similar to the one she had seen in Thomas' house. *But, there was nothing there a moment ago. I swear I'm losing my mind.* She breathed the words under her breath.

The book opened on its own accord as they approached. Thomas circled around to the far side of the desk and leaned on the edge. The book began to project as they approached. Hovering and spinning above the page was the image of a middle-aged man. His hair was wild and stringy, and it stuck out in every direction from under an oversized top hat. He lounged on a pile of cushions, his head thrown back in statuesque laughter. He certainly looked harmless, even welcoming. The lights flickered, sending them back into darkness for a few seconds before resuming a gentle glow. The image in the book, however, had changed when the light returned.

The man on the cushions had been replaced by two figures hovering around a desk. When Alex looked closer, she saw that it was Thomas and her, standing around the same desk that separated them. They simultaneously whirled their heads around looking for any sign of a camera, but only found darkness. If Alex hadn't felt the ground beneath her feet, she might have thought the whole scene was floating in the vacuum of space. Their eyes locked, both their jaws were set, sure that something wasn't right. Again, the light flickered, dropping them into darkness. Seconds later the light was on and the two of them stared down at the book in front of them. This time, however, Alex could only see herself standing beside the desk. She looked up and Thomas was still staring across from her.

"Why has the image changed so only I'm there?" Thomas questioned. Alex shook her head in confusion. It wasn't Thomas standing by the desk. Surely the long hair was a dead giveaway.

"Don't be ridiculous. That's clearly me."

"No... Tha-." His argument was cut off as the lights flickered again. Only it didn't sound like hesitation, it sounded like his voice had been sucked away into the vacuum. When the light returned, Alex looked across at the empty space where Thomas had been moments ago. She called for him, but he didn't answer. Silently she listened for any sign of movement, but the cave was as void of sound as it was light.

Flicker.

The book flipped around, facing the other way. She watched as it was pulled by an unseen force toward the edge of the desk.

Flicker.

The book slammed shut. It flew across the desk toward her, and she jumped back. Her heart raced. Something was in the cave with her.

Flicker.

A stone with jagged edges lay in the middle of the desk. Scratched in the wooden surface was an arrow pointing toward the back of the cave. The light remained constant, and she was left in the dim light alone.

She looked at the darkness in front of her and sucked in as much of the musty air as she could handle, trying to resolve herself to the task ahead of her. Pushing her way past the desk, she forged forward. She had to find Thomas. After only a few steps, the entire scene changed as fast as she could blink. A corridor lit with torches on each side appeared around her. Instead of mossy cave walls, the new walls were carved with intricate designs. Along the right side, the images were of a short fat Queen adorned with a heart in the center of her chest, sending her army forward. People knelt on their hands and knees, crouched over stumps as men with long axes held them aloft. It was a terrifying and ugly scene.

Not all the carvings, however, were terrifying. Along the left side of the corridor, there was a much different picture of Wonderland. Rich gardens with roses so delicately carved out of the stone ran along the wall. Alex thought for a moment that she could reach out and pluck one of them away. The scenes morphed as she moved forward. Each new scene was framed by beautifully carved ivy, leaves twisting and bursting out of the wall as if they had grown into place. There were images of small cottages surrounded by lush forests, people working in gardens, happy and proud under the sun.

Obviously, she was confused. How could such a brightly lit corridor simply appear out of the blackness? Why hadn't she seen it from the entrance of the cave? She spun around to examine the cave. Instead, she was met with a thick black and seemingly solid wall. She placed her hand on it, but it passed through into the inky black and disappeared from view. She looked back at the corridor then stepped through the black threshold. Sure enough, the desk was still there, lit by the lamp, book open in the middle, as it had been when Thomas and she had found it. Walking over to it, she could no longer see scratches in the surface. Everything had been reset. A million questions raced through her head as she returned to the brightly lit hallway. Somehow, Oothro, whoever he was, had figured out how to make a light containment field. Her father would have been ecstatic to see such an invention.

In front of her, she noticed another arrow scratched into the hard flat stone of the floor. It said *A, this way, T.* Why had they been separated?

As she traveled along the corridor, the pictures on the walls unfolded much like Thomas had told the story a few days earlier. The Red Queen was lying in bed, ill and dying. The Black Queen rose to power in a great revelation of sunbeams. The images surrounding the coronation were joyous and individual frames marked carvings of specific inventions. However, the scenes soon turned darker. The bright, joyous celebrations morphed into a mural of a wall being erected around the city. City folk from the outer districts clamored over each other to get to the edge of the wall, only to be pushed back by guards. Another showed the Queen standing on a platform, her head held high, as the other finely dressed people cheered at their new fortunate situation.

The next showed a large ring; matching the one the Queen had constructed to harness the power. On one side of the ring stood a lush and prosperous forest. On the other side of the ring, the land was parched and barren. Carvings of burned trees and poisonous vapors rose from the earth. Whoever carved these images didn't seem to approve of the Queen either.

Along the left side of the corridor, the images continued in an opposite fashion. Alex couldn't decide if they were depictions of a time that had once been or hopes for a time yet to come. As the people gathered into towns and cities, they worked together to erect buildings. There were similar advancements as the ones on the previous wall, only instead of a great ring of power, there were fields of windmills, and what looked like solar panels on roofs. There was still technology integrated into the society in many ways, but the people all seemed to coexist on an even playing field with each other. Instead of the Queen ruling from above, every carving seemed to show a simple man. His face was different in every scene, but in each he wore a top hat that towered above the crowd. In every case, he worked alongside others to erect structures, reveal innovations, and move forward into new eras. In each story, he stood just ahead of them but on the same level.

At the end of the corridor was a single door. Its dark oak finish was elaborately carved with vines and flowers. There was no doorknob to be seen, and a dark screen was inset at its center. She pushed on the door, but nothing moved. On the floor, sets of numbers were scratched, but instead of the neatly laid out path that

Thomas seemed to be leaving her, the sets of numbers seemed to mean nothing. They were upside down, backward, and in multiple mismatched sets of five. Feeling around the edges she tried to push her nails into the crack but had no luck in moving it. She slapped it with the palm of her hand in anger and the screen sprang to life. The words that illuminated the screen were in intricate script.

The Queen of Hearts has invited five guests to her royal banquet. She has assigned a seating arrangement for each guest, but unfortunately, she can't remember where she placed them. Can you help her figure it out?

The five guests are the Knave of Hearts, the Duchess, the Caterpillar, the Mock Turtle, and the Gryphon.

1. Each guest is seated at a different position around the table, numbered 1 to 5.
2. The Knave of Hearts must sit next to the Duchess.
3. The Caterpillar must sit next to the Mock Turtle.
4. The Gryphon can't sit next to the Duchess.
5. The Mock Turtle must sit at position 3.

Can you determine the correct seating arrangement for each guest? Be warned, you will have only one attempt

# to submit the correct response.

Under the text appeared the image of a table. Five characters appeared next to the table, each matching the description written above. The seats were laid out around a circular table. Each seat was labeled one to five starting at the top.

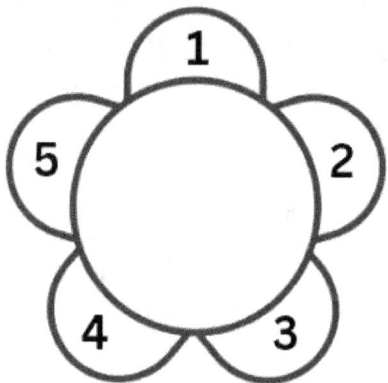

Alex touched the screen to test how it worked. She placed her finger on the icon she assumed represented the Mock Turtle and moved it into position three at the table. It shifted slightly as it dropped into the spot matching the seats outline.

Looking at the four icons left. *The caterpillar must sit next to the Mock Turtle.* She read the line to herself again and moved the caterpillar token into position four. Even though it could also fit in the number two spot she had to start somewhere.

*Since the Knave and the Duchess have to sit next to each other, that should put them in spot one and two.* With a swift motion she dropped the duchess in spot one and the Knave it spot two. With only one spot left she quickly dropped the Gryphon in spot five. With all icons placed, a submit button appeared on the side of the screen and she moved to press it with urgency. *Check your work.* This time it was the voice of her mother that echoed in Alex's ears. She had always rolled her eyes at the reminder, but something about not hearing her mother's voice in several days made her pause.

Glancing back at the seats she saw her mistake almost instantly. *The Gryphon can't sit next to The Duchess. Of course!* She shuddered to think what might have happened if she had pressed submit. Quickly switching the Duchess and the Knave she now had her answer. The Knave of Hearts sat in 1$^{st}$ position followed by the Duchess, the Mock Turtle, The Caterpillar and the Gryphon. Reading over the rules of the puzzle a final time she was satisfied that she had chosen correctly.

Her finger punched the submit button and the door came to life. The wood carvings that covered the door receded like vines shrinking away from the sun. The door slowly disappeared with them leaving an opening and the continuation of the corridor. A few meters ahead she could see it split off in two directions. Before she had time to react, a figure rounded ahead of her and entered the corridor from the left.

# TARGET ACQUIRED

"Alex! You made it!" Thomas' voice echoed through the passage. "I was beginning to wonder if I'd lost you for good."

"Thomas!" Alex exclaimed in response, "Where did you go? How did you get ahead of me?"

"Well, I figured out fairly soon that they had split us into two dimensions. It seemed clear that they didn't want us to work together on the last puzzle. Of course, I've been studying the technologies in Wonderland a little longer than you, so I figured I'd leave some clues."

"Actually, I was able to see your arrows, but there were at least twenty sets of numbers listed at the last door." She laughed. "It doesn't matter. I'm just so happy to see you again." She flung her arms around him. At first, the hug seemed like an embrace of relief, but it didn't take long for butterflies to flutter around in her stomach. She wanted to let go, but she was compelled to stay pressed against him. He was stronger than she had imagined, and his body was warm. He responded with his own lingering embrace as he breathed in the scent of her hair. In unison, they both lost their nerve and almost cast each other away. The silence between them was awkward until Alex finally broke it.

"So, where do we go next?" Her voice echoed against the walls.

Thomas snapped his focus back. "Right, I've been in both directions; it appears there are doors on either side with switches. One of the doors is orange, and the other is blue. I've tried pressing the buttons on both sides, but nothing happened."

"Okay, so we each take a direction. Maybe with more time we can puzzle it out, divide and conquer as they say." she suggested.

"Right, but then what? What if we get split up again?"

"Well," Alex nodded in contemplation, "I think that the goal is to get people to the end, and if one of the doors were dangerous, there would be another puzzle to work out. It's worth a try, we can meet back here in ten minutes to relay what we find."

"That makes sense I guess," Thomas agreed, but seemed reluctant to part ways with her again. After a beat he nodded and without another word the two of them headed in opposite directions. As Thomas had described the door in front of her was orange. There was a glowing beam of light around the entire frame of the door. A single red button was on the wall. The surface of the door was smooth and cold, as she ran her hand over it before pressing her finger against the button.

The door zipped open and disappeared into the frame. In front of her was a room with two glass walls and a black stone floor made from the same material as the replicators. In the center of the room was a rack, complete with two guns. Both guns were adorned with glowing glass tubes in the center of them. Thomas appeared across from her, his door whizzing open at the same time as hers. Dual triggers! They must have had to press the buttons at the same time. Alex marveled at their luck.

The wall at the back of the room was made of a chalky white stone wall. The last wall was missing entirely. From the edge of the platform, where the missing wall should have been, it appeared that the floor was suspended over a cavernous, seemingly bottomless pit. A second platform lay approximately forty meters across the chasm. Alex and Thomas examined their only route forward. Around the corner, barely visible on the other platform, was another door, surrounded by blue and orange bands of light.

"This looks familiar for some reason." Alex mused allowed, but she'd never been to Wonderland so she couldn't fathom why. "He's not going to make this easy... is he?" She turned to Thomas.

Thomas was a bit more gleeful about the realization than Alex would have liked. He picked up one of the guns in the rack, its central tube glowing with a soft blue light, and pointed it at the glass. Alex ducked, protecting herself from the flying shards of glass she was sure would be the result. There was, however, no large crash of glass. Cautiously she peeked through her fingers.

"Are you crazy?!" she reprimanded. "You can't just pick up a gun and shoot it!"

"Well, I figured," his sly smile never left his face as if he knew something Alex did not, "he wants us to get to the end so if there aren't clues, we can't be in any real danger." He winked.

Alex hmphed at the use of her own words against her in argument. "That's not exactly what I meant..." before she could finish, he pointed the gun again at the ground and pulled the trigger. Again, nothing happened. Without missing a beat, he pointed at the white chalky material along the back wall and fired. A large circular hole, filled with glowing blue energy appeared before them. It revealed nothing on the other side. In fact, it looked like a glowing splotch of paint in front of them. Alex glared at him slightly before walking over to the wall and touching the blue spot. There was an energy signal to the quivering blue circle, but the wall was solid. She pushed against it, but nothing happened.

"Hmmm... I wonder." Thomas pondered as he pointed the gun at the chalky white wall on the second platform. The instant he pulled the trigger, an identical blue splotch showed up on the wall on the other platform. The energy radiating onto Alex's hand disappeared, and when she looked again at the wall she was touching, the blue splotch was nowhere to be seen.

It dawned on her where this was familiar. She remembered an old retro game her father had played with her a few lazy Saturday mornings. *Why would a video game from Earth be set up as a test in Wonderland? Perhaps there have been more people traveling from world to world than the queen realizes.* With a smile and wink at Thomas she picked up the gun and pointed it at the back wall, pulling the trigger. "Alright, let's get this party started?"

Alex took a running jump through the glowing hole in the wall. She almost laughed as she watched him panic as she landed on the other side of the room. He had run after her and was now ringing his hands.

"Hey!" She hollered at him. "Are you coming?" He whirled around, almost toppling over as he spun. She couldn't see his face, but she was sure a puzzled look adorned it. She saw him shrug then march over to the hole in the wall. The puzzled look still covered his face, and she confirmed her suspicion that it was, in fact, very cute. She couldn't help but be a little proud that she finally knew something in Wonderland that he didn't. Reunited, they smiled to each other as they realized what they had discovered. The door opened and revealed another room beyond.

As in the last room, this one had various platforms and cavernous drops. The door seemed unreachable on the other side. The floor to the platform they arrived at was ended abruptly by a bottomless pit. Above them, the ceiling was higher than before. Most of the room was made of black stone, except for one white surface far above them; on the wall, close to the top of the room. The other platform was twenty meters directly across from them and was covered in a mossy green cushion. Without indicating her plan, Alex shot an orange splotch onto the ground in front of them, at the edge of the platform. She looked at Thomas, almost challenging him to figure out her plan without her telling him. He half smiled back, accepting her contest. Seconds later he tilted his head, the answer clear in his eyes as they locked hers. Without a word and without looking away he aimed his gun at the surface above the mossy platform. His portal opened as it had before. Together, they leapt into the hole in the floor, their hands grasped as they plunged.

A second before landing, the adrenaline high of figuring out the puzzle wore off and Alex realized that running, jumping, or landing were never her strong suit. She suddenly wished she had paid more attention in gym class. On landing, Thomas rolled easily to a standing position, as if jumping and rolling had been part of his genetic makeup. Alex, on the other hand, was grateful for the mossy cushion. She wasn't, however, lucky enough to survive unscathed. Her ankle twisted on landing, sending shots of pain coursing up her leg. The cavernous room filled with her cries, and she pulled her knee to her chest. It took every ounce of courage she could muster to keep from crying, but she knew there was no time to waste. There was no way back, and she would have to move forward. She had come this far, and, at this point, her curiosity was bubbling over. How important was this man that he needed a vast array of security puzzles between him and the entrance?

"Are you okay?" Thomas' eyes had softened. She nodded, hardening her resolve against the pain. His concern surprised her as he pulled off his cloth belt and wrapped it carefully around her ankle to stabilize it. "Can you continue?"

"I don't know what choice I have." Her words were more biting than she had intended. She was still mad at herself for letting it happen in the first place. The remarks seemed to cascade off him and he placed his arm around her, helping her stand.

The rooms continued to get more complicated. As she remembered doing in the virtual world on Earth, they disengaged buttons with hidden weights, directed lasers at mirrors, and disarmed drones as they traversed the maze of puzzle rooms. They were beginning to think the rooms would never end when they came to a room larger than the rest. Its vastness gave the impression of a final test of their abilities and combined all the components they had just traversed to this point.

A series of levels worked their way up to a door approximately one hundred feet up on a platform above. Directly beside them coming out of the wall was a blue energy field, flat and straight. It looked like a floating walkway and stopped at the white wall opposite them. On the second level a laser pointed at the far wall. Next to the beam, a mirror sat on the floor and a target lay on the wall, ninety degrees from the beam's origin. On the third and final level, two drones, encased in glass, hovered back and forth, although they didn't appear to be able to see the lower levels. A barrier extended from the wall, blocking the drones from seeing each other, and Alex could make out a barely visible white square in the center of it. She aimed her gun, holding it as steady as she could and shot an orange dot on the surface above.

"Might as well take the easy way out." Alex shrugged. Thomas pointed his gun at the white wall across from them, opening a portal to the top level. Immediately, one of the drones spotted them through the portal and sent a barrage of lasers at them. Alex hadn't expected the drones to shoot through the glass, and she felt Thomas' weight as he pushed her to the ground. Her injured ankle contorted, and she could no longer hold back her tears. As soon as they were hidden from sight, the lasers stopped. Thomas' shoulder was bleeding, and the skin was singed. The smell of burnt flesh filled the immediate area. Luckily, the laser had cauterized the wound enough that the blood only trickled out of him. Alex disengaged her opening, which made the drone benign for the time being.

"We're going to have to take out the drones."

"Ya think!?" Sarcasm oozed out of her. She was frustrated and angry at the rash decision that had almost killed them. Thomas, however, chose not to acknowledge the icy-cold words.

"Let's take it one level at a time." He walked over to the hovering energy platform and placed his hand on it. The touch seemed to confirm his suspicion, because he hoisted himself up onto it, and was soon standing in mid air. Alex joined him, but not before she shot a hole into the platform directly above them. As expected, the moment they opened the portal in front of the floating walkway it extended forward allowing them to walk across. They inched forward, careful not to attract the attention of the drones above them.

The next platform proved to be simpler. After testing the beam to see if it was safe, and coming back with a fried boot, Alex cautiously stepped over it and made her way to the mirror on the far end of the platform. The target was on the left wall and glowed a brilliant orange, matching the colour of the beam. Alex carefully tilted the mirror, directing the beam into the center of the target, unsure what to expect. A rumbling began above them, causing them to duck and cover before scanning for the source. A wall directly between the drones began to recede. The second the wall was no longer blocking their view, the drones opened fire on each other. When they had both tumbled to the ground Thomas and Alex hugged each other. This time, the extended embrace was deliberate on both sides. Alex nestled her head into his shoulder and drank in his scent. She crinkled her nose a little, because the smell of sweat, no matter who's, was still a bit gross, but something about him was still intoxicating.

Reluctantly they broke their embrace; with the drones gone, their exit was easy. Alex looked at the final level of the room, and with the center wall gone the only white surfaces she could see the back walls of the cages that had encased the drones. Thomas shot his gun toward the far wall and waited for Alex to open her portal on the wall next to them.

"No," she responded. "It won't work. If we go through there, we'll be trapped behind the glass."

"I know, but perhaps there's a way out up there?" It was hard to see the platform, but she squinted, and could see nothing but flat walls beyond the glass.

"That can't be it." Alex looked at the room, trying to find some other way onto the platform above. There were no other white surfaces leading toward the platform, the walls were all made of black stone.

"I don't see-"

"Wait!" she exclaimed, pulling him toward the floating walkway. She nudged him toward the entrance they had come from and made her way to the mirror. It only took a small movement before the orange beam was no longer pointed directly at the target. As she had hoped, the wall from above began to protrude from the wall, returning to its original position. They made their way back to the entrance and waited. When the wall had come to a stop, Alex shot her hole in the wall, in the same place she had hit when they entered the room. This time, there were no drones to shoot at them from the other side of the wall. They walked through the portal, across the beam and hopped down onto the ground next to the exit. Looking at each other, they shrugged as they simultaneously placed their hand on the button to the next room.

# FAILURE

The door opened into a forested clearing. It wasn't what either of them had hoped for or expected, but at least they were outside again. As they stepped through the door, it disappeared completely. Directly in front of them was a miniature version of the three ominous rings that had been destroying Wonderland. These ones, however, were much smaller than the three that caused so much death and devastation. They were as tall as Thomas, but unlike the larger versions, they lacked the yellow and orange pulsing energy field within their interiors. They examined the area, trying to discern what the miniature power plant might be fueling, but found nothing but trees as far as their eyes could see.

"That was a waste of time." Alex teetered on a nearby rock as she tried desperately to elevate her throbbing ankle. Thomas' ever-present optimism seemed to be waning as well. He sighed and sat, visibly exhausted, next to Alex, and rubbed his head.

"It just doesn't make sense, why would anyone create an elaborate set of tests only to spit you back out into the forest again. It seems ludicrous." His words were filled with more contemplation than complaint.

"Tests?" Alex's suspicions had been confirmed, but she wondered at Thomas' assured assessment. "What are you not telling me?"

"Nothing." He hesitated. "I just mean… they seemed like tests."

"Maybe we failed?" Alex offered, letting her suspicion rest for now. As if on cue, a humming sound filled the clearing. The rings that had previously seemed inactive lit up and a glowing yellow-orange field stretched across the inside of the circular containment ring. Each of the smaller rings began to glow red, spreading an orange hue between the areas. She would have taken a picture if she hadn't dismantled her phone. Her time in the dungeon seemed like ages ago. The sudden surge in energy, however, was too peculiar to ignore. Moving forward, each of them once again examined the bottom of the power device, trying to discern its purpose. As they examined, the humming noise increased. The orange hue spread, and the ring began to pulsate. Around the ring, the grass and moss began to dry up and burn away. The decay was spreading quickly, forcing them back.

"I think we need to get out of here."

"Agreed." The two of them turned and made their way in the direction they assumed was West, but, at this point, any direction would do. About ten paces later, Thomas was knocked backward. Alex recognized the momentarily pixelated screen instantly. Cursing, Thomas rubbed his nose and moved northward instead. Another ten paces and, once again, he was met with the restrictive projection that imprisoned them. Leaving his hand on the wall, this time, he moved along it as Alex limped behind him. A false backdrop surrounded the entire perimeter, but there were no indentations or indications of a doorway. His hands clamored for the door where they had just come but it too seemed to have disappeared into the backdrop. Thomas looked up, examining the upper edge of the trees. He breathed deep, taking in the intoxicating scent of the forest. They were clearly outside because they could feel the breeze on their faces, but there was no way to tell how tall the wall was, and it would be a waste of time with Alex's injury.

With no way out, Thomas turned his attention to the tiny generator in the middle of the room. The decay had slowed as it made its way outward, but it continued to spread as the field drew power from the sun. The focus circles on the lower left and upper right were glowing a molten red, and Alex was surprised that the whole thing didn't melt away. The yellow that was once present had morphed into a bright orange, and the hotter the device became, the more the ground disintegrated.

"We have to shut it off." Alex finally resolved. "It's the only way, somehow we have to turn it off."

"It's not that simple." Thomas was annoyed with her lack of

understanding. The patience he once displayed had morphed, and his face was now covered in worry lines. He began to pace, closing himself off from her, rubbing his head and neck as he berated himself. Alex could see that a solution would be up to her. Obviously shutting down the generator would be hard, nothing had been easy, but there had always been an answer.

"Look," Alex began to puzzle her thoughts out loud. Only a tiny glimmer of hope that Thomas would listen remained, but, at least, he would hear her if he managed to pull himself out of his bubble of self-criticism. "All generators have a source of fuel, turn off the fuel source and the generator would cease to function."

"It's impossible, the fuel source is the sun! You can't just turn off the sun." Clearly, he hadn't been as detached as she thought. He was, however, shooting down her ideas with no alternatives of his own, which infuriated her.

"Listen," she snapped at him, "If you're not going to help then I'll kindly ask you to Shut… Up..!" She hadn't meant to shout, but she needed to focus.

"The power source, as my genius companion, so kindly pointed out is the sun." her sarcasm rang through as she continued, "We can't just turn off the sun, so how do we keep the generator from receiving its energy."

"We blot out the sun," Thomas' voice was less oppositional. The bait had worked.

"Right," she confirmed, "but blotting out the sun, barring some other catastrophic world-altering event, isn't that easy." They both stared off into the fake forest for a while.

"That's it!" Alex exclaimed as she watched as the shadows danced along the ground, the canopy of the forest providing some comfort from the sun. The forest around the larger generator had burned away, giving it less shade and ultimately more power as it continued to store the energy in critical mass. Thomas stood staring at her, waiting for her to share her internal epiphany.

"Right, sorry, we need to construct something, something that will blot out the sun long enough for the power to dissipate." Looking around, she tried to find some building materials. Luckily, the forest between them and the wall still provided some shade. Before she could voice her idea, Thomas was already breaking branches off nearby trees. He pulled at as many of them, still lined with leaves as he could. Alex joined in, finding brush and branches off the ground. After fashioning a square frame large enough to cover the device, they worked to fill the frame with foliage. When the makeshift shade was sufficient to block out all the sun's rays, they decided to try it out. Alex strained as she tried to push it up over her head but could barely sustain it for much longer than a few minutes. It had quickly become much too heavy for her, and they would have to come up with a different shade material.

The spread of decay had slowed substantially as they blocked out the sun. Luckily, the effects hadn't spread too far. However, if they were anything like the real thing, the material of the rings was strong enough to withstand ten times as much power as the generator was currently emitting, and soon it would continue to ramp up and burn the entire room, including anyone left in it at the time.

Thomas removed some of the branches, thus removing the weight keeping them from their goal. After a few tests, they finally found a weight that Alex could bear for an extended period. Unfortunately, it left a drastically large gap in the center of the shade. Their conversation was minimal, restricted to requests for help securing a branch or the need to have something handed to them. Now it was Alex's turn to show a sign of defeat. She was exhausted, her ankle was throbbing, and she was out of ideas. Perhaps they *were* doomed? She collapsed onto her back, huffing from exertion as they placed the shade back on the ground.

"It's no use. I'm not strong enough to hold what we need to block out the sun. There's nothing else we can do. Like most things, you would have been better off if someone else had come along. I'm just a liability." She fought back her tears by closing her eyes. The hot sun beat down on her face as the humiliation of being inadequate washed over her. Suddenly, the warmth of the sun disappeared and was replaced by a cloud of darkness. She opened her eyes to see Thomas leaning over her.

"There's no one I'd rather be stuck here with than you. You're brilliant, resourceful," he stroked her cheek, catching the stray tear that managed to sneak out, "and not to mention beautiful." Leaning in, he touched his lips softly to hers. His lips were so soft, and she could smell cloves hovering in the air around him. The heat inside her rose substantially, and her heart began to flutter. Her hands were immediately filled with pools of sweat as everything inside her flashed with energy.

"If you're quite finished with admitting defeat," he untied the leather thong holding the top of his collar together. His loose shirt was buttoned at the front, and he made his way to the first button, undoing it. After he had reached the second, Alex bolted upright, jolted back reality by what she thought was about to happen.

"Oh my god...no... wait... I'm not ready for this... I know we're going to die soon, but...I..." the words spilled out of her in a flurry, gaining momentum the longer she spoke. Thomas just continued to smile at her as she pushed him backward, getting back on her feet. His hands continued to make their way down his chest, revealing his muscular torso underneath. Alex averted her eyes for a moment but eventually gave into the tingling urges building inside her and turned back to face him. Instead of moving toward her, however, he moved toward the completed shade. In a few moments, he had the shirt secured over the gap and ready for implementation.

*Of course!* She thought, *how could she have been so daft.* He must have been appalled as she blabbered on about what she thought was going to happen. Mortified, she moved to her side of the shade and stared at the ground.

"Don't worry, we'll talk about *that* when we aren't about to die... trust me." She looked up at him and his grin was almost as wide as Ches's had been. He winked at her and the heat of embarrassment inside increased further. As soon as their shade was over the glorified battery, its colour changed from a bright molten red to soft orange. Their plan was working! Neither of them was sure how long it would take for the tiny power plant to disengage, but they stood there, arms raised, staring into each other's eyes for several minutes.

She let her mind wander; trying to avoid thinking about the burning pain in her arms. She had never held her arms in the same position this long, never mind having thirteen kilos of weight bearing down on them. She swayed from side to side, and just when she thought she could not bear it any longer, she watched the field inside the circular ring wink out. The shade toppled to the ground with a crash, almost catching Thomas in the chin. They watched as tendrils of smoke rose from the heated ring, threatening to light the shade on fire, and Thomas quickly flung the constructed wall of kindling aside. The sky above had disappeared. Instead, a bland grey ceiling stopped about six meters overhead. As they had predicted, the room was also about six meters wide and six meters long, encasing them in a perfect cube. The ground was dirty, and the various trees that surround them appeared to be real enough. Someone had gone through a lot of trouble designing this little test.

Alex looked around for some means of escape and was ecstatic to see that another door appeared along the west wall. Judging by the earlier surprises they had encountered, she was beginning to think it was safer to stay put, but with no way back, they moved forward. Thomas was at her side, his shirt returned to its original position; singed spots and all. She grimaced, bracing herself, as the door creaked open.

# LIES

What awaited them on the opposite side of the door was the most startling thing they had encountered thus far. The room erupted in cheers as the two of them stepped through the threshold, and Alex plugged her ears against the thunderous applause. The circular room was cavernous, at least thirty meters in diameter. Ledges and balconies had been cut out of the walls, each leading back toward what Alex assumed must be a room or hallway. The flat floor of the cavern was still original stone. It appeared to be a place for congregating and eating, and by the sound of echoing cries, everyone was congregated. Hundreds of people dotted the balconies and filled the main hall. *Was this an underground city?* If it was, Alex judged that this must be the central square based on the number of people congregated. She wondered how many winding networks were cut into the earth. If it was a city, it looked as though it had been there for years. However, it wasn't nearly as crude as she imagined and an ancient city cut into stone, deep under the ground might be.

Drones buzzed and whizzed between tables carrying trays of food. However, these drones didn't have lasers and whips. Instead, they used their tentacles to fill beverages and season food. There were orbs floating around the room as well. Some carried large loads from one area to the next, and others were fitted with cameras for surveillance. The cavern was full of technology. Food replicators stood in a line along the wall. Hologram tables showed views of the surrounding forest. Everyone in the crowd wore a PCD, but these models looked like they were a few versions past any she had seen so far.

Not everyone in the crowd was a stranger. Ches leaned against the far wall; her Cheshire smile as big as ever as she casually scanned her nails for dirt. A pristine white android, identical to the ones in the castle, stood at the front of the crowd. The only difference between this one and those at the palace was his common brass gears. Next to him, a short, wiry man in a forest green suit jacket and matching top hat vibrated with excitement. The top hat was fitted with a set of goggles, like the ones in The Park, but these looked much older. The metal frames around the lenses were carved with curling designs that traveled off the metal and into the leather that strapped them around the hat's middle. The man's face was thin and gaunt, his aged skin slack. His eyes and smile, however, showed a kindness that masked his age, emitting a childlike aura. The long-curled mustache that stood out at each side of his face also helped to soften his bony features. Despite his apparent age, his agility matched that of a teen as he strode forward, almost skipping, and clapping his hands.

"Congratulations! You did it!" His voice was squeaky and reminded her of Mr. Hart, who lived next door. He was always cheerful and happy as he waved goodbye to her every morning. The last few months, she had gone out of her way to avoid his over optimistic greeting, but after the last few hours, she was grateful for some optimism. "Most people give up at the desk, they close the book and try to walk away. This opens the shortcut of course. Everyone wanting to join is welcome. You took the challenge though!" He said the last part so everyone in the cavern could hear, and the crowd roared again.

Thomas and Alex looked at each other with the same 'what the hell' look. "We could have taken a shortcut!?" she said curtly.

The small man raised his hand and the crowd stopped immediately. A serious expression settled on his face as his voice echoed through the silence. "You must be very clever to get through all the puzzles." He eyed them with suspicion, and Alex's heart began to race. The man's face grew grave as his eyes bored into them. The two of them were backing toward the door when the man burst into uproarious laughter. In response, the entire crowd burst out into laughter. He laughed so hard that a snort came out of him as be doubled over. Even after the crowd had lost interest in the joke, he continued unrelentingly for longer than was comfortable.

"You... hahhahahaa... you should see... oh goodness...

hahahahaha… the look on your faces!" Suddenly his laughter stopped and a kind smile under his ridiculously curled mustache once again welcomed them. "Welcome to OOTHRO!" he motioned around him to the cavern beyond.

"Wait…Oothro is a… place?" Alex looked puzzled. She looked around the room and back at the tiny man as he tilted his top hat further to the side.

"Yes yes… Order of the Hat's Rebel Outpost. Oothro." Hearing the words rebel outpost, Alex immediately shot an accusatory glance at Thomas. Had he known all along? He did say his parents were part of the rebellion. He responded with a prolonged shrug; a crooked smile accentuated his plea for forgiveness. Anger bubbled up, and she had to bite her tongue to keep from berating him in front of everyone. Narrowing her eyes, she hoped he would understand her frustration. He had lied to her! Why hadn't he just told her the truth? Before she could retaliate further, the man clapped his hands again.

"You must be hungry," he giggled, "We should have tea! Tea is the answer to everything, you know, that and forty-two, but you can't do much with forty-two, so I say tea!" He moved toward the other edge of the cavern, obviously expecting the pair to follow. The others in the area had dispersed, and the cavern was only half as full as it had been upon arrival. The man muttered nonsense for a few more minutes while they made their way through what remained of the crowd. Everyone stepped aside, letting him through with a nod of appreciation or reverence. When they reached the other side of the cave, a tunnel opened and the man stopped.

"WAIT!" the sudden outburst made Alex jump backward knocking into Thomas. He tried to steady her, but she shook him off, still upset by his apparent dishonesty. "I never introduced myself! How silly of me! I'm The Hat!"

"The Hat? Like the Mad Hatter?" She almost laughed aloud herself but managed to stifle her amusement so only a few giggles made their way out. In an instant, it all clicked. He was, however, immediately annoyed with her laughter.

"It's *The* Hat!" he protested, staring her down until she lost her amusement. Once she was silent, he burst into his own bout of laughter.

"Works every time." He laughed, when he had cleared the tears from his eyes he continued walking as he spoke; "No one has called me the *Mad* Hatter for," he stopped to think, "oh at least since the time of The Queen of Hearts. I suppose image is all marketing anyway."

# T.E.A

They wound their way through a series of hallways cut out of the rock. Glowing sconces lit the way with a soft yellow light. Doorways dotted the halls, each with an access panel set into the stone beside it. The very last door in the corridor was larger and more ornate than the rest. Alex recognized the swirling pattern from the goggles on the wiry man's top hat. The door slid open as Hat approached.

Inside the room, sunlight streamed in through large openings in the far wall. A balcony led outside and Alex could see water rushing over a ledge above them. The entire wall was open to the rushing water, and judging from the lack of noise or breeze, they were protected by energy windows. Inside the room was cozy. It was decorated similarly to the cottage they had found in the woods, only there were several rooms leading off the main one. In the center of the room was a grand sofa, carved out of wood and upholstered with a multi-coloured quilt that matched the one on the bed in the cottage. Two chairs flanked it and a large coffee table, or rather... tea table, sat in the center. The same ornate display of teapots and teacups covered the surface. The plates were stacked high with cakes and cookies. Hat motioned them to sit, and they obliged.

"You must be Thomas." Hat said matter-of-factly as he poured three steaming cups of tea. Taking a flask out of his coat pocket, he poured a luminescent purple liquid into his own cup. "You have your father's jawline and your mother's nose."

Thomas sat up straight, taken aback by the mention of his parents. A wave of grief washed over him as he was reminded about his recent loss.

"Why so glum?" Hat patted him on the shoulder. "Drink up!" the man guffawed. Alex shot him a warning glare, eyes as wide as she could. He ignored her and continued to chuckle.

"My oh my," he continued, "You two are a melancholy pair."

"You would be upset too if you had just lost your parents!" Alex snapped. She couldn't sit back and let this man continue in such a cavalier manner.

"Lost your parents? Oh dear, my child, I'm sorry to hear that." He directed his comment at Alex.

"Not me... well...not now... it doesn't matter." She threw her hands up in frustration, almost toppling a precariously perched cup.

"Why certainly you don't mean..." The Hat looked at Thomas, shocked. He jumped up and beelined across the room. He leaned into a communicator on the wall and mumbled a few sentences that Alex was unable to hear. The two of them looked at each other in confusion, Thomas still despondent. Hat skipped back across the room, a gleeful smile plastered across his face. Alex was about to stand up and leave; she had had quite enough of this ridiculous, silly, leprechaun.

"Just as I suspected. Leniva and Jaysen are still safely tucked away undercover at the castle." He smiled at Thomas, who was disoriented at the news he had just received.

"But, how? Why wouldn't they tell me?" Thomas probed.

The Hat just sat back and sipped his tea, his mustache twitching as he swirled the beverage across his tongue. He appeared completely relaxed now that the matter of Thomas' parents was settled in his mind. "Secrets must be kept if you are ever to win against the enemy." He gingerly placed his hat on the floor and promptly pulled the tea cozy off the pot and placed it over his head. "Never trust a man who, when left alone in a room with a tea cozy, doesn't try it on." He continued to speak through the knitted material.

She had never felt as bold but she felt that Thomas deserved an explanation. Alex burst out. "Have you..."

"Have I gone mad?" Hat cut her off, finishing her sentence for her. He tittered. "I'm afraid so, but let me tell you something; the best people usually are. When you've lived as long as I have, you end up going, at least a little batty along the way." The tea cozy was off and back on the pot faster than either of them could blink. His

Einstein-style hair splayed out wildly before he placed the hat back on his head.

"How old are you?" Thomas broke into the conversation. His voice was resigned and relieved. He was obviously frustrated and elated at the news of his parent's whereabouts, but clearly didn't wish to discuss the matter further.

"One hundred and eighty-seven." Hat responded confidently. "I know, I know, I don't look a day over eighty." He puffed out his chest and tilted his head back. His top hat threatened to fall off his head, but he caught it, forcing his white hair to splay sporadically out from under it.

"How is that possible?" Alex wasn't sure that anything was impossible anymore based on her experiences the last few days, but Hat certainly didn't look as old as he claimed to be. In response, he patted the chest pocket where he had stowed the flask from earlier.

"I fancy myself a bit of an Alchemist. It's amazing what happens when you combine ingredients from different worlds together." Before they could question him further, he set down to business. "Now that we have enough members of our team capable enough, we can carry out TEA."

"Tea?" Thomas asked, "Isn't that what we've been doing for the past half an hour?"

"Oh No! I mean T E A, the Tactical Energy Act." He pressed a button on the arm of his chair. Alex hadn't even noticed the button, but as she scanned her own chair, she noticed that several of the carved designs were movable. The table in front of them sank into the floor and a new surface grew out of the table legs that were left behind. The surface bore the familiar grid shape of a hologram table.

The scene sprang to life as Hat relayed his plan. "The plan is to leave as soon as the sun goes down tomorrow. Our only hope of saving Wonderland is to shut down the power rings. By shutting down the main source of power we leave the castle mostly defenseless. As you've recently heard, we have operatives on the inside that will open up key entry points before the power goes down. They have gained the trust of the court and have been waiting patiently for us to proceed. As you found out, the rings will turn off if deprived of fuel for long enough." An image of the rings sprang forth from the table, each of them pulsating with bright red energy. Four zeppelins flew in with one corner of a large sheet of balloon material attached to each of them. The shade's colours matched the multi-coloured style that Hat was obviously fond of. Thomas and Alex watched as the zeppelins flew over and positioned the large shade over the rings. "The plan is to position the shade before the sun comes up. With their power source gone throughout the night, the rings will already be at their lowest power levels. They can last the night, but it will only take about an hour into the day before the rings are dormant and unable to restart without help."

"What does this have to do with us?" Thomas sat back on the couch taking in the scene as it unfolded. He crossed his arms over his chest as he asked the question.

"Well, you're the final piece to the puzzle! The final members of our team."

"What!?" Alex and Thomas proclaimed in unison.

"We have been waiting for two more with just your skill set. Luckily you came at the same time. Now that we have a team assembled, we can move. You'll join the team assaulting the ground."

"Whoa, whoa, whoa," Alex protested. "I didn't sign on for a ground assault. I just want to get home. I'm not here to join a rebellion."

"Oh?" The Hat looked surprised then continued disappointed, "Well, if that's all you want, then I suppose it can be arranged." He twirled and curled his mustache. Thomas looked as disappointed as The Hat did. As the plan was being revealed, Alex could see the look of excitement and craving for adventure creep onto her friend's face. She had never fancied herself as brave, so the thought of joining a rebel attack on a radioactive solar base wasn't her idea of a walk in The Park. However, as she thought back on her adventures since she entered Wonderland, she realized that she had already done more than she would have ever dreamed. Perhaps she wasn't as incapable as she thought.

"Where do you get your power?" Alex was suddenly curious. "It seems like you have a lot of your own power requirements. Are you not drawing from the grid?"

"Oh, a fabulous question! I love clever girls." The Hat was once again giddy. He walked over to the balcony, motioning them to follow. When the energy field was removed, the sound of rushing water was almost unbearable. The water roared over the ledge and a mist covered their skin the instant they left the interior of the dwelling. Hat moved to the edge of the balcony and pressed a button on his PCD. A new energy dome formed over them, protecting them from the spray of the waterfall and blocking out the noise. However, a full view of the surrounding area revealed itself. They weren't underground as Alex had originally expected. They were, in fact, almost a hundred meters off the ground standing on a balcony carved into a cliff face. Along the rocky surface, several more dwellings and balconies covered the cliff behind the waterfall. The waterfall was huge, it plunged down creating a choppy white froth at the base. Beyond the froth, more dwellings, built on stilts and what appeared to be completely natural materials surrounded a large lake by equally high cliff faces.

"We have a natural power source of course. The waterfall provides all the power we need without the need for storing and creating unnecessary overloads. However, we have also managed to use the grass blanketing the top of our cliff. It's amazing how much energy plants can harness from the sun, and they are often more than willing to share if they are asked nicely. We provide them with tending and nutrients and compost, and they send their extra energy into our grid. We have more than enough power here to last us ten times over. Anything that we don't use is just put back into the natural environment around us at no risk." The Hat beamed.

"How did you come up with all this?" Alex continued.

"When you've had a hundred and eighty-seven years to ponder and create, you can come up with a lot of things young lady. I don't expect you to understand." He let out a final sigh. "Well, I suppose we continue our quest for a new member." He turned and moved back inside his rooms with Thomas close on his heels. Alex stood, staring out at the spectacular natural city that lay in front of her.

"Wait," Alex called after them in a small voice, still unsure if she wanted to complete the thought that had sprung to her mind. The two looked back questioningly. "I'll do it." Her words were final, as much to convince herself as the two that were staring at her.

Hat clapped his hands in glee, and sat back down in his chair, "Now! About that ground assault!"

# CLONES

The next day was a whirlwind of preparation. Everyone else in the complex had had an abundance of time to take in and understand the plan. Even Thomas caught on quickly, but Alex was having a hard time wrapping her head around her role. She was to be part of the team that disabled the ground defenses. If the zeppelins were shot down, then there would be no hope of shutting the machine down. Everything depended on perfect timing, and their ability to disable the key defenses. Not only that but they had to sabotage the main power grid connector to prevent the rings from being powered up again once they were down.

The night was approaching, and they had been outfitted in black leather outfits. Their shoes were lined with the same black rock that made up the replicators and walls in the puzzle rooms. It made their feet very heavy, but it was supposed to protect them when walking across the radioactive field. Each of them was given a ventilator that fit over their nose. She placed it in her mouth and breathed in deeply. The air entering her lungs was like an open field of daisies. Finally, she was given her own PCD. It would, of course, serve as the main source of communication between the members of the team and the airships. The ground team's devices, however, had a few upgrades that might prove handy, including a grapple, portal capability, and the ability to link into the main computer network. The best thing, in Alex's mind, was the vaporizing gun. She hoped she wouldn't have to use it on anything living, but it would certainly even the playing field against cyborgs.

They had been given a tour of the airships. Their tour guide rattled off a list of facts about the impressive ships as they walked down the hall toward the observation deck.

"The material for the balloons was my own design. It's interwoven with a special obsidian fiber. Obsidian fiber you ask? Wel…" Alex stopped listening when the door whooshed open and the ships appeared in front of them.

The giant vessels looked ready for the sea and straight out of Narnia. However, the large zeppelin like balloons strapped to their masts served as a much different type of sail. The huge ships hovered in the air beside the waterfall and Alex wondered how she could have missed them when they first gazed upon the city at the bottom of the falls. People busied themselves on the decks loading crates and adjusting cannons. The cannons, however, weren't what Alex had imagined for the ancient looking ships. Lights blinked from panels beside them and the deck of the ship looked more like the Enterprise than the Dawn Treader. Alex could have stared at them all day, but the tour was ended as the guides voice trailed off in the distance and Thomas tugged at her shirt.

Their next stop was outfitting. They were each given dark clothing, and their pants were covered in more pockets than Alex knew what to do with. She reached in a few of them and stopped after the first few revealed contraptions she knew she wouldn't have much hope in understanding. There was already so much to learn and remember, she didn't want to bog herself down with more than was necessary.

Once they were finally outfitted, they were to be briefed with the other two members of their team before going out. Alex was nervous to meet the others that had managed to solve the puzzle rooms. Thomas sat beside her in a large boardroom where they waited. The conversation was minimal, as they both focused on the insane task ahead of them when the door swished.

Ches walked in first, grinning ear to ear. She winked at Alex and nodded her hello. Behind her, the robot followed. Its solid white cover plates had been replaced with black ones, assumingly to provide cover. Apparently, they would have some of their own robotic power accompanying them on the mission. Alex peered past them looking for the fourth person to join their party, but the hall was empty, and the door closed.

"I guess we're waiting for one more?" Alex turned with a puzzled smile.

"We're all here." Ches nodded confirmation, "We should get started."

Alex looked around the room, puzzled, before she felt Thomas' hand on her shoulder. She looked at him, confused and saw his look of acknowledgment.

"Pleased to make your acquaintance," the robot voice still reminded her of C3PO, "I'm Rab." She took his hand and shook it. It was surprisingly human-like in feel compared to how it looked. Rab's face was shaped like a human's face, only it was clearly made of a synthetic material. As he spoke, his features moved fluidly the same as flesh and blood would. His eyes had a surprisingly human look as well. Even with no hair, he was eerily lifelike. His head was attached to his torso by a series of wires, poles and cogs that weren't constricted by the cover plates, presumably for ease of movement. Similarly, the rest of his joints were exposed, with his major mechanics safely undercover.

"Oh," Alex back peddled slightly, "I thought we would be taking another real person on our team." She turned to Ches. "How did you program him to seem so real?" Ches laughed and Rab's smooth eyebrow line crinkled together as his eyes formed an irritated stare. The hue on his cover plates started to turn red as he began to speak.

"I assure you, while my intelligence is *artificial*" he emphasized the word, clearly uncomfortable with the term, but resigned to it, "I'm almost certain it is greater than yours. While I don't expect you to understand my *differences*, I can tell you that I too was born, have a father who loved me very much, and I am likely more committed to this cause than you are." By the time he finished his speech, his colour had changed completely to cherry red.

"I'm sorry!" Alex pleaded, trying desperately to take back the offense she hadn't meant. "It's just that I saw more, just like you, at the castle, and they weren't like you. I mean… they looked like you, but they were different, they didn't say…" Alex watched as his colour changed once again from crimson to white, and back to black. He closed his eyes as if he was centering himself and nodded in understanding as she stammered on.

"It is understandable how you might get confused. Please excuse my outburst. I have worked hard to convince everyone here that I am in fact on their side." He paused, seeing on Alex's face that she could use some more explanation. "When the Queen first took power, I was happily working with my father as an inventor in his shop. We created things that people needed, but I had so many more ideas that, at the time, I felt weren't appreciated. My father wanted me to focus on things people requested, instead of the things I felt they needed." He lowered his head, closing his eyes for a second as if remembering someone he had obviously lost. Alex recognized the look immediately.

"When the new Queen was crowned," Rab continued, "she had such an appreciation for the new. She asked for volunteers, and people who could bring the kingdom into a new age. The Queen of Heart's tyranny and oppression made her sister's new leadership feel like new oil in the cogs and blinded us all. Of course, a hundred years can taint a person when they have the power of a kingdom behind them."

"One hundred years?" Alex interrupted, "But the Queen hardly looks over twenty."

"One of the things I'm least proud of." He hung his head in shame. "I was excited to see a Queen who valued invention as much as I did. I left the shop, against my father's wishes, and headed to the castle. She let me present my ideas, giving me free reign. I suppose she felt that she had won the jackpot. I was able to create many things I thought would help the kingdom, and many of them did. The PCD you wear on your arm was my invention. I created drones and robots that could perform the most menial tasks for people, allowing them the freedom for fun and relaxation. I also created the virtual reality screens and goggles that you've likely already seen if you've been to the castle. I never intended them to end up as they have."

Alex remembered the strangely disappointed stares that had been present on the faces in the courtroom as people were jerked out of their own personal worlds and into the real one. Their goggles had linked directly with their temples, she finally understood, creating the interface. She wondered how many hours they spent just sitting there, completely isolated from each other in their own virtual reality.

"I was even excited when I proposed the new energy source to her. It would harness the power of the sun, helping to make the generation of power move from coal and mining to a renewable source. If the ring had been used as intended, with only the taxation it could handle, it would still be working to this day." The last statement was disappointed and defensive, even though no one was directly blaming him. Ches rocked back on her chair, patiently waiting for the tale to end. Thomas nodded here and there aware of the history but as interested in the lesson as she was.

"The people of The Park petitioned for more segregation. After all, they felt themselves to be superior. By the time Lindzel ordered construction of the walls, she no longer needed me to build things for her. I had created an unstoppable workforce of drones and worker robots for her. The walls went up, and the ring began to fail. It became so overheated that it was beginning to emit solar radiation and burn the surrounding forest. Fires broke out, which she kept controlled at the expense of many lives from the lower city. She ordered the creation of another ring, and when it was erected, the destruction continued to spread."

"But that wasn't enough for her, was it?" Alex asked, the picture of everything finally forming in her mind.

"No, the people of The Park wanted more and more. They each wanted their own little mansions, to the point that even married people with families each had their own tower dedicated to each member of the family. The more they desired, the more energy was required."

"That still doesn't answer my previous question. You said she was over a hundred years old? How is that possible?"

"Right, I was just getting to that." His piercing stare met her directly in the eyes, and she had to look away.

"The Queen began asking for things I was uncomfortable with. When she asked for something that would keep her young forever, I told her it couldn't be done. In all seriousness, it *can't* be done. Human cells can't last that long. However, cloning *is* completely possible." Rab stood and walked across the room. He pressed a button and the whiteboard screen that had been blocking the entire back wall disappeared and revealed the back of the waterfall. They were on one of the lower levels, and Alex could almost see the frothing junction where the lake and waterfall met. Rab stared out the window for a few minutes before continuing.

"I refused at first of course. I had seen the damage that was being done, but she answered my defiance by taking my father prisoner.

He was old by then, and he had stopped being the chief inventor in the lower city many years earlier, when the use of technology became prohibited to anyone living outside The Park. She made me watch as she tortured him, and I gave in quickly. My father begged me to resist her, saying he was old anyway, but I couldn't. He was still my father, my creator, and I still loved him." Alex was surprised at the mention of love. She hadn't thought that artificial beings were capable of love. The look on Rab's face, however, seemed to prove otherwise. He stared out at the surrounding lake for a long while in silence. Alex placed her hand on his in support.

"The problem with clones is that they each have their own experiences," he continued at the recognition of her touch, smiling slightly at her in thanks. "If you're grown in the lab at an accelerated rate, you have no history to draw on. This is apparently exactly what Lindzel had wanted because her next request was to devise a way to transfer her consciousness into the new body. She was already over thirty by this time, and her new body appeared as young as the day she was crowned. She craved the rejuvenated beauty and forced me to accelerate my research. I had heard whispers that she was also becoming weary of my lack of commitment, and she knew that my father was not long for this world, and soon she would be unable to control me."

"Once she was safely stowed in her new body, she rose again victorious in front of her followers. They were excited about their Queen's rejuvenation and longed for their own chance at the treatment. Luckily, the Queen is the greediest of them all, and she refused to share this with them, as far as we know." He turned to face the room, leaning against the wall, the window behind him forming a brilliant cascading backdrop.

"And the Cyborgs? Were those your inventions too?" Alex was suddenly curious about some of the more ominous treatments people had been subjected to in the castle.

"Fortunately, my conscience is clear where some of the atrocities lay. I might have been the fastest inventor, but the Queen had commissioned hundreds of others from the city. Even some of the people in The Park, with a vested interest in the safety of their *families,* were involved. Once I left things became even more grave."

"How did you leave?" Alex prodded him.

"As I said, she was growing tired of my opposition, so she had me create replicas of myself. She ordered that these new androids would have allegiance to only her as their creator or mother. I knew I couldn't do that. If I created androids with the same ability to adapt and grow as I had, and gave them over to her as their dark hearted mother, the world would be doomed."

"However, I couldn't refuse outright. My father had fallen ill, and he was still a captive. I wasn't yet prepared to lose him, so I created her robots. I even transferred by intelligence into them, at least, the knowledge I had already had. If they seemed at all different, she would be alerted to my plan. I did, however, leave out the ability to grow and adapt. They were loyal to her, but they would never be more than robots programmed with knowledge. They talked like me, walked like me, and even knew what I knew, but they lacked artificial intelligence. However, it wasn't as easy as I first thought and it didn't take long before she realized my ruse. Luckily, under the cover of night, I incapacitated the guards, and took my father with me. I ran into the cover of the forest, carrying him. I had heard of a group of rebels, and wanted my talents to be remembered for something my father would be proud of."

"So you found Oothro, and have been working with them ever since." Thomas finished the story for him.

"Yes, that was, at least, twenty-five years ago."

"Right!" Ches chimed in, her cheery voice cutting through the sullen and somber mood in the room. "Let's get to work shall we?"

Now that they had returned their focus to the operation, they plotted their route and finalized their plans. They talked well into the afternoon and finally stood as the sun began to disappear.

# HOLD ON!

Alex lowered her body into the sidecar beside Thomas. The shiny black motorbike looked like the fancy racing bikes of her own world. The main difference was that this one ran on water instead of fuel. The team split up, approaching the facility on flanking sides. The scouts had been able to bring back intel about some of the defenses, so they had some idea of what lay ahead. The first obstacle would be a maze, accessible on both sides. They would have to find a series of panels, and all would need to be shut down to disable the energy shield that surrounded the rings. After that, the instructions were vague.

The two-wheeled vehicles made no engine noise as they rode through the forest toward the waste except for the occasional crunch of leaves and twigs under their tires. Periodically they had to avoid patrols, but that was easy enough. Lack of opposition had made the patrols complacent. From her sidecar, Alex watched the night go by, wondering what she had gotten herself into as her stomach churned. It was too late to turn back, so she tried to set her thoughts on the task ahead.

When they finally got to the waste, the two vehicles split and silently entered the charred radioactive field. If the intel was correct, they wouldn't encounter anything for at least a few kilometers. The night was starless, but the moon was full. A faint glow from the previous day's energy was still lighting up the rings and the area around the facility. They could see it easily on the horizon, and would have to contend with how bright it was when they arrived. For now, the cloak of night hid them from any onlookers. The entrance to the shield maze would be guarded by cyborgs, but Alex and Thomas had already decided on distraction as a tactic to get past them. Everything seemed to be going fine until the smell of burning rubber reached her nostrils. Looking down, she could see the rubber wheels of the sidecar giving off tendrils of smoke. The further they progressed, the larger the smoke plume became. They hadn't taken into consideration the superheated ground. Panicked, she grabbed Thomas' arm, almost making him lose control, and wordlessly communicated their situation. Thomas cursed.

"Hold on!" She heard a crackle and his voice came through a speaker in her helmet. The bike sped up, faster than it was ever intended, and the noiseless quality disappeared. In the distance, she could hear the other bike accelerating as well. The noise from the bikes seemed to attract attention and a set of blue lights rose on the horizon. When they were about five hundred meters from the facility, Alex could see glowing blue cannons had risen out of the ground. As if they had been waiting for the right moment, deadly beams of light streaked out of their gun barrels. Thomas weaved back and forth, avoiding the fire. They hadn't anticipated this!

"Shoot them!" Thomas' words were less of a command and more of a desperate plea.

She had never aimed and shot at anything in her life that wasn't a game. How was she supposed to get rid of laser guns? Shakily, she raised her PCD, pointing it forward. Taking aim, she turned her gun to vaporize and pointed it at the nearest turret. Touching her index and thumb together, a force of energy shot from her forearm, jerking it backward. The blast didn't come close to its target. Instead, the ground in front of them disappeared, leaving a large hole. Thomas veered sideways trying to avoid it, and the two of them almost toppled over onto the poisoned earth as the back wheel of the sidecar hit the hole. She tried again, but each blast fell short. When she did manage to connect, only a few were incapacitated by her efforts. There had to be another way. By now the entire facility would be on high alert, and the entire plan threatened to crumble in front of them. Everything Oothro had been planning, depended on them...on her...and she wasn't fond of the pressure. That's when the idea struck. She pressed a few buttons on her PCD and aimed.

Touching her middle finger to her thumb, this time, a tiny blue circle appeared on the wall of the shield maze, it was still so far away they could barely make out it's features. A few seconds passed and her ring finger contacted her thumb. This time, her target was much closer. An orange circle opened, and a bright light poured out of the ground. Thomas understood. He drove the bike into the open portal and out the wall of the complex. Apparently, the turrets could only shoot and sense one direction, because once they disappeared, the firing stopped. She assumed the others had found cover as well.

The smoke from the tires was thick, choking them and clouding everything around them from view. Luckily, it was also clouding them *from* view because the familiar stomping of metal reached her ears. As quickly as they could move, the two of them jumped from their seats and hid behind the bike. The ground here had been covered in cement, probably to protect the guards from the corrosive ground. The cyborgs had activated, and through the occasional break in smoke, she could see that their guns were already drawn. So much for the 'distract and sneak' method. She felt Thomas lift her helmet off and grab her shoulders. His face was a lot calmer than she imagined hers was. Everything in her told her to run, run as fast as she could, and maybe they wouldn't see her. It was too bright to find cover in the dark, and she would have to contend with the turrets if she ventured back out into the field. Maybe if she was quiet enough.

"You can do this!" Her scheming was interrupted by Thomas' reassurance. His voice shook her out of the daze that had grappled her. The wide eyed panic that covered her face was replaced with a steely glare.

"You take the one on the right. I'll take the one on the left. You'll get one shot, make it count." Looking through the smoke, she could see the black armored machine moving toward them. It wasn't in a hurry, but it showed no signs of wavering. She readjusted her PCD and stretched out her arm over the bike to steady it. Clenching her muscles as tight as she could, she braced herself for the force of the blast. Her fingers twitched before making contact, and she closed her eyes at the last second. She waited, counting the seconds as she clenched her eyes tighter. Instead of certain death, she felt a soft hand on her forearm. She hadn't realized that she was still clenching her muscles tightly, and the touch of her companion let them release, causing her to collapse on the ground. The smoke was dissipating, but the smell of burn rubber still filled the air. She had hit her mark, and both guards lay in a pile of black metal shavings.

She grinned broadly at Thomas but they had no time to revel in their glory. They would be safer inside, and they were on a deadline. Thomas pulled her toward the entrance, and she didn't have to be reminded twice to follow.

The walls directed them through the first few turns in the maze, but their luck didn't last long. They arrived at their first junction three corridors in. There was no roof on the maze, so the light from the rings lit their way. It was, however, hotter than either of them had anticipated. They had been given a few cold packs in case of overheating, and their water cans were full, but it didn't take long for beads of sweat to form in places that Alex didn't know she could perspire. The junction in front of them had three possibilities; they had to be methodical, or they would miss some of the control panels. Their Intel told them they would find twelve. Alex and Thomas were to take care of six, then meet Rab and Ches at the central exit leading toward the facility.

"I took the liberty of writing a little program and uploading it to all our devices." He took her arm and pressed a few buttons. Their previous path showed up on the device. Four glowing dots blinked onto the screen as well. Ches and Rab were moving quickly, and they had already revealed twenty-five percent of their half of the map. Two red squares showed up in corners of the maze, and Alex assumed that those were control panels that had been disabled.

"We should split up," Alex suggested.

"Are you sure?" Thomas touched her wet forehead. His fingers lingered a bit longer than expected and Alex was thankful that she was already flushed from the heat so he couldn't see her reaction to his touch.

"I'll be fine. I'll find you." They darted in opposite directions, weaving up and down every corridor they could find. With the map of the maze in front of her, it was easy to navigate. Her first box showed up after only a few turns. A waist high, black stone cube lay tucked against the wall. There were no access panels that she could see, and no buttons or levers appeared. A single green light blinked on and off at the top of the box. On her knees she scoured the ground, looking for a power source, but also came up empty.

According to the intel, the box should have had a panel attached. Activating her PCD she spoke aloud.

"Thomas?" Static. She slapped her device. "Thomas!?" The screen began to flicker and the map was threatening to disappear. Her heartbeat skyrocketed. She kicked the block of stone, stubbing her toe through her boot, and cried out.

"Think Alex! Think!" She scolded aloud. What would her father do? What would Thomas do? She came up blank. A voice in her head chimed in; it sounded like her mother.

"*What would Alex do?*" it asked. The voice was right. She was the only one that could solve this problem. Glaring at the box, she circled it, raised her arm, and took aim. The box disappeared into a pile of shavings, and a red blip showed on her screen.

"Well, that worked." She said aloud.

Thomas had taken care of two in the time it took her to find and destroy one. The heat bore down on her as she ran through the maze. She managed to find and destroy two more devices and there was only one more to go. She rounded the corner and spotted it seconds before Thomas rounded the corner on the other side. Both took aim at each other in defense before recognizing their ally standing before them.

"I got this." She confirmed, and she watched him take off toward the central facility. Once the final box was destroyed, the blue energy field disappeared in a wave. She followed her companions, who according to her PCD, were already waiting for them.

They found them crouching behind the wall, discussing their options. None of the spies had penetrated the defenses this far, so they had no idea what to expect past this point.

# WELL... THAT WAS FUN

"Well! That was fun!" Ches welcomed them with her usual smile. She was casually leaning against the wall, tossing a stone in the air, and stalking it with her eyes on the way down. Thomas had an exhilarated grin on his face. Clearly, he was having as much fun as Ches was. In fact, Alex was beginning to wonder if she was the only terrified one in the group. Rab was mumbling calculations to himself as he worked out the next phase of the plan.

"It appears there are at least twelve turrets around the building. Their focus is aerial assault, as they overconfidently assumed that no one would get through the ground defenses." Thomas chimed in.

"We'll take the perimeter; you guys head inside." Ches dropped the stone and joined the conversation. Everyone nodded in agreement and the four of them cautiously stepped through the opening and into the courtyard. They collectively held their breath, expecting to jump back behind the barrier, but when nothing happened they bolted. The door to the facility was unlocked. Rab was correct, the Queen's forces were extremely confident in their outer defenses.

The cold air inside the facility was a welcome relief as they stepped inside. The room they found themselves in was no larger than a typical entryway, but it was completely enclosed and windowless. The only light came from a single gap, twice the width of a doorway and blocked by the expected energy field. An access panel glowed on the wall. Through the energy field, they could see their prize. A giant orb of fire hung suspended in mid-air at the center of the room. It looked like a miniature version of the sun, but the flares jumping off it resembled lightning instead of fire. The tiny sun was contained by a cylindrical shield, and a circular console with hundreds of levers and buttons surrounded it. The gauges and output screens cast their information holographically, and waves of energy spiked up and down as the glowing orb churned and discharged against the shield. A single thin stream of energy was drawn downward into a jet black cylinder under the tiny lightening sun. They had all expected it to be a harder task to find the storage console, but it looked as if Lindzel had opted for convenience. Alex puffed her chest out and smiled. The sense of victory was a rush she had never felt. She was a hero, and she loved it. They strode forward in unison.

It took her a few moments to register the feeling of falling as the panel in the floor opened and Alex and Thomas plunged downward. The edges of the chute had been smoothed and lined with metal, reminding Alex of the waterslide park near her home. Their descent continued at a furious pace as they slid through the darkness, twisting and turning in a tangle of bodies. It seemed to take forever when, suddenly, they were flying. The freefall lasted only a few seconds and the damp she had been missing from the slide was replaced with a splash. The cavern they found themselves in wasn't large, but it was filled with a constructed pool of water, presumably to catch intruders in the makeshift prison. Along the far wall, a small entrance opened into another tunnel leading upward. Several piles of bones lay strewn about the cavern where other intruders had perished, presumably starved to death.

Why hadn't they climbed the tunnel? Confused by their lack of escape, Alex pulled Thomas toward the exit, knowing there wasn't a second to spare. They had to get to the console above and destroy the storage device before the guards took control or they would be able to turn the rings back on. Her body bounced backward as she crashed against the crystal-clear piece of glass. Stifled laughter echoed from behind her and she glared at the ground. Refusing to look back, she rubbed her face and righted herself, tending more to her bruised ego than her wounds. Before she had time to pity herself further, the sound of chattering filled the air. It sounded as if thousands of tiny metal hammers were tapping at the same time. Out of a series of holes at the back of the cave, emerged hundreds of mechanical metal spiders. Alex screamed, jumping backward against the glass wall. Spiders! Why did it have to be spiders! Frozen, she watched as the mechanical arachnids skittered forward. They had always been her greatest fear. While Thomas blasted them, she stood frozen. His blaster made minor holes in the wave of metal arachnids, but the tide continued to rise. She could vaguely hear him calling for her to help him, and although she had imagined many ways of dying over the past year, death by mechanical spider hadn't been one of them. The sound of blasting and tiny metal legs clicking across the floor filled her head, and then, everything went silent.

# LET'S TRY THIS AGAIN

When she opened her eyes again, the sea of spider bots was still rushing forward. It was as if no time has passed at all. However, in a few seconds, Alex and Thomas would be ripped to shreds. Courage flooded her. She turned toward the glass barrier. After a few quick shots, she grabbed Thomas by the collar and dragged him through the portals just as their pursuers reached the edge of the cave. As she closed the portal, a few stray spider bots trickled through, but in seconds they were a pile of metal dust. The others crashed angrily against the glass, the sound of cracking caused them to bolt around the corner and out of sight. After a few seconds, the bots stopped their pursuit, and all became silent. Peaking around the corner, they could see that most of the creepy bug-like robots had dispersed.

They proceeded down the tunnel as cautiously and quietly as they could while remembering the immediacy of their task. The tunnel rose quickly, and the crudely carved walls turned into perfectly chiseled stone corridors. Periodically, pieces of the wall had fallen away, leaving small piles of rubble and stones scattered along the walkway. The floor had been carved in places as well; symbols and patterns adorned some of the flagstones. Why would someone go to all this trouble to decorate the tunnel to a prison? *Perhaps they went down to observe the prisoners being eaten alive from time to time,* Alex considered as they made their way upward toward the next phase of their mission. They pushed forward quickly, so when Thomas grabbed her arm to stop her, the jarring motion almost winded her.

"Ow! What the hell?" she complained.

"Look." He pointed to the floor at one of the decretive

flagstones. Like many of the others, it was about two meters long and took up almost the entire width of the corridor. It had a spade, surrounded by swirling ivy adorning it, the symbol of the Queen.

"Ya... so what?! We already knew that the sadistic Queen is behind this facility. Come on, we must hurry!" She tried to push forward but he stopped her again.

"Traps." Thomas' voice was grave. "Look closer."

As she examined further, he pointed out what he had noticed. One stone wasn't connected to the rest. Instead, it had a tiny gap surrounding it. She watched as he examined the rest of the corridor. The stark passage bore sconces on the wall, giving off a faint light for them to see by. She followed his eyes to the ceiling, which was completely flat, but directly above them about a meter ahead were a set of holes in a perfect line.

"I thought this was becoming too easy." Alex couldn't contain her sarcasm, and Thomas smiled a little at her joke. "What is it?"

"Let's not find out." Thomas squeezed himself against the wall, walking along the only edge that wasn't occupied by the decorative slab. They slowed their ascent, taking care to examine anything that looked out of place. With the slower pace, Alex contemplated her vision in the cavern. Had it really been her father? What was he trying to tell her? Why would he show her a memory from her childhood? Most of all, she wondered at his statement about the end being the beginning. All her questioning amounted to no answers. There were several more slabs, bearing the Queen's symbol, which they easily avoided once they knew what they were looking for. The corridor stopped abruptly. The hall ended with a flat wall with three sconces adorning it. They examined it for any cracks or seams but found none. As far as they could tell, the entire corridor simply ended here, as if the entire underground tunnel system was a cruel joke designed to instill hope in anyone who managed to get past the legion of spider bots. Together, they pushed against the solid wall, but nothing moved. There wasn't even a hint of shifting. Thomas began to pace.

"Why?! We've come all this way! They were counting on us!" he yelled at the walls. Alex knew his anger wasn't directed at her, but she stepped back uneasily. He leaned over, picked up a stray piece of crumbled wall from the floor and threw it at the dead end. As the stone bounced from surface to surface, it ricocheted off one of the sconces. Instead of breaking, the sconce let out a long harmonic tone, which shocked Thomas back to attention. The surprise on his face matched her own.

Alex moved toward the wall slowly and tapped on another sconce with another stone she had picked up along the way. Similarly, this sconce let out a long harmonic tone, but its pitch was slightly different from the first. Thomas was already beside the third, and as he struck it the third note with a slightly different pitch from the first two.

"What purpose could this possibly have? Something to entertain us as we starve?" Thomas said, still puzzled, with biting sarcasm still present in his voice.

"No!" Alex exclaimed in revelation, "It's the key!" Before he could question further, she began hitting the sconces in order, ringing out a musical tune as she went. By her calculations, there were only six possible variables to the key, assuming it only had three tones. Starting with the first, she changed the order that their music filled the corridor. On the third combination, the wall in front of them faded away revealing the room they had first arrived in. The glowing orb of orange lightning was now half the size it had been. The airships must be in place, the power was waning, which meant that the guards would be upon them shortly.

The room seemed clearer as she examined it. Flashes of her vision sprang into her mind as she looked around the room. It was almost identical to the one she had seen when she was five. Thomas was pulling levers and pushing buttons, but nothing seemed to influence the energy stream or the glowing orb. Walking over to the console she calmly stood next to Thomas, knowing exactly what needed to be done.

"Turn off the shield." It wasn't an order, but she was as sure about her request as any she had ever made.

"Are you mad. If we turn off the shield before we deactivate the power connection we have a very good chance of being cooked."

"Trust me." She looked him directly in the eyes, waiting for him to comply. Her determination seemed to be enough for him because he walked over to the other side of the console and began working with the controls. In the meantime, she readied herself. Stretching out her arm to take aim.

"That won't work. We can't just blast it. The material is made of a different composite, you risk blowing the entire facility! You might have a death wish, but I don't!" Thomas had stopped his work to lodge his complaint. The comment hit her hard. For the first time in a long time, she didn't have a death wish. The realization hit her like a punch in the guts. She stared at him, shoulders braced against his arguments, but her look of determination unwavering. After a few seconds of staring, he broke eye contact and continued his work. She had adjusted her PCD and waited for the shield to deactivate.

Once it was down, she tightened her finger on the trigger. The grapple sailed through the air, the target coming ever closer. Her eyes watched the trajectory as it seemingly wavered back and forth. This was not the time to miss. She held her breath as time seemed to slow. The grapple hit the side of the cylinder that had been collecting the current. The glass teetered back and forth momentarily before tipping off its stand. The stream was interrupted, bolts of lightning began to shoot in every direction around them.

"RUN!" Alex yelled as she bolted for the door. Thomas was right behind her. They avoided the false floor and slammed the door behind them, running as fast as they could for the shelter of the maze. As they reached the wall, a large explosion erupted behind them, shooting them forward. The force of the blast had whipped her head back, and it felt as if her brain had smashed against her skull. The last thing she remembered before the world went black was watching Thomas, lying on the ground beside her. Blood dripped down his cheek from a wound on his head. She wondered how much damage had been done to her by the blast, but at this moment, couldn't bring herself to care. Thomas reached out, grabbed her hand, and smiled before closing his own eyes. Blackness enveloped her.

# SWEET SORROW

She woke in a brightly lit room. It looked like Hat's quarters back at Oothro and her immediate view was open to a waterfall, confirming her suspicion that she had somehow made it back at Oothro. Rainbows danced in the sunlight and bounced on the walls around her. She groaned as she tried to sit up.. Every wall was lined with comfortable beds and side tables, and most of the them were occupied. One of the attendants of the room was standing at a central counter filled with beakers and bubbling concoctions. People groaned from their beds as caregivers scurried around tending to their wounds.

"Hello?" She croaked out as she rubbed her head. The woman looked up and bustled over.

"Don't try to talk dear. You've been asleep for a few days. It will take a bit to get your voice back." She handed Alex a glass of purple liquid. It smelled sweet, and Alex was parched. The cold liquid somehow warmed her insides. She was immediately revitalized. Even her minor aches from her long sleep seemed to fade.

"There you go. Feel better?" The woman smiled before she walked away. As she left, Alex saw her speaking into her PCD.

Alex pushed the covers aside and noticed her clothing had been replaced with a pair of fuzzy pink pants and matching t-shirt. They were the softest pajama she had ever worn. She walked across the room and looked down at the city below. Somehow it looked even more beautiful today than the first day she had seen in, and she wondered if they had succeeded. The empty feeling she had when she looked around for Thomas and didn't see him was also unexpected The thought of him seemed to summon him because the door whooshed open.

She didn't wait for him to reach her, she matched his strides, weaving between beds and people. She narrowly missed a woman carrying a platter of purple vials. They collided in an embrace.

"Oww!" their voices rang out in unison, then laughter followed. Apparently they needed a bit more time to heal.

"Did we win?" Alex asked. "What about the castle? Did The Hat make it in? What happened to Ches and Rab? What about the Queen? Did they catch her?" The questions poured out of her so fast that Thomas didn't have time to respond to any of them.

The door opened again and a small man bounced forward, his top hat teetering back and forth with every skip. "You're awake! How wonderful! How wonderful! You must have questions." He paused with a smirk, "Real tea this time?"

Hat walked to the waterfall edge of the room and sat in a group of chairs that Alex had presumed were for visiting family members to wait. The table hissed and several cups of tea with a plate of cookies appeared.

"Brilliant work by the way." He motioned for them to sit with him. "What made you think of disabling the power conduit?"

Alex didn't answer. *A vision of my dead father told me what I needed to do?* Instead of answering she shrugged. "Lucky guess?"

Over the next hour, Hat described how Ches and Rab had successfully disabled all the turrets though Rab had to replace an arm when he returned to the base. This allowed the ground assault to get closer to the facility and ensure that no one could repair the turrets.

"The airships had come under heavy fire, despite their efforts to disable the ground defenses. Guards had poured in on all sides, and the Queen's army had drones on their side. They were aiming for the balloons, but luckily, nothing could penetrate the obsidian-enforced design." Hat explained. Ches and Rab and several members of the air crew joined them as they listened.

"Once the crew had managed to down all the tiny drones, they could focus on helping us on the ground." Ches chimed in. "Just when they had thought the battle was lost, your little explosion on the ground caused the distraction they needed to turn the tides.

"We thought we were done for," one of the crew members said, "but that explosion gave us the opening we needed."

Ches had nodded. "Let's take advantage of it and finish this."

"The forces at the castle had a harder time. While they had been able to seed the guard and the servants substantially, the core city defenses were much more robust than anyone had imagined. The Queen managed to hack some of Rab's programming and what we thought were bumbling mediocre copies of our friend here," he motioned to Rab, "were quickly converted to killing machines. That combined with the cyborg army made things much harder than we expected."

As Hat relayed the story, a woman entered the hospital room. She looked identical to the picture Alex had seen on the side table the night she stayed with Thomas.

"We had many casualties," Hat looked at Thomas and his mother and paused a for a few moments of silence, "but their sacrifice wasn't in vain. The castle team also succeeded. Sadly, the Queen slipped away in the confusion but we now have control of the city."

"She got away!" Alex seemed more outraged than the rest of the room.

"That will need to be a battle for another day." Hat responded calmly. Alex huffed.

Thomas and his mother gave each other a downhearted but contented look that Alex recognized from the days after her own father had died. A pang of empathy tugged at her heart and she resisted the urge to wrap her arms around him.

"So…. what happens next?" Alex chimed in. "Do we search for the Queen? Will the people in Oothro move into the city? What about The Park and the outer city? Who will be in charge? Do you take over?" Again, the words flowed out of her mouth like lava.

"Well… a lot of the answers we don't know yet. We will have an election and allow the people to decide who will lead them into the new era. As for everyone here, they will go about their lives, and decide for themselves what path to follow next." He paused. "And what about you? What's next for our hero?"

Alex had never been called a hero before, the feeling was astounding. She had made so many friends in Wonderland, and she loved it, despite almost dying several times. What would be next for her? She was terrible at making decisions. She gazed at the view and then back to Thomas. His mother hugged him close as a tear travelled down her face. Alex thought of her own mother.

"I think… I want to go home," she said the words hesitantly, looking at Thomas, pleading for him to understand. It was hard enough convincing herself that she wanted to leave her only friend in all the worlds behind, and she didn't think she could refuse if he asked her to stay. Thomas had become more than a friend. Her heart ached at the thought of leaving him, but each time she glanced at Thomas' mother, she was reminded that her own mother needed her too. No matter what lay at home waiting for her in her own world, she had to face it. Besides, if she stayed she'd likely be a distraction and Thomas' mother would need Thomas now more than ever. Thomas didn't protest, though she could see the sadness in his eyes.

"If you're sure." The Hat's usual giggling demeanor disappeared and his broad smile morphed into a solid line. His eyes, however, still twinkled as she nodded her agreement.

"Yes," she said with finality.

"Very well then!" He jumped up, his energy returning instantaneously, and bound across the room. A small vial of dark purple liquid was wrapped in his hands when he returned. The colour matched the berries she had seen in the forest on their journey to Oothro. Instead of plain blueberry colour, however, the liquid was glowing as brightly as it had the night she first encountered the plump berries.

"The secret," he gave her a knowing wink, "I harvest them at night." She looked away embarrassed before taking the vial.

Alex looked over at Thomas who stood. She walked over and softly wrapped her arms around him, resting her head on his chest. This time, neither of them let the awkward teenage embarrassment keep them from enjoying the moment. This would be the last time they would see each other. He let her hug linger, his own arms squeezing tightly, as if not wanting to let her go. When he broke his embrace, he tilted her chin to see her tear-filled eyes.

"The end is only a new beginning." He mirrored the words she had heard her father say a few days before. Stepping back, she took one last look at the crowd that had gathered and swallowed the glowing purple concoction.

# FRANKENGIRL...

The room was empty when she woke. A curtain had been pulled around her for privacy, and she could hear another patient in the bed next to her coughing. She tried to sit up, but couldn't move. In the hall she could hear nurses bustling about their daily activities, talking about their lives, and their plans for the upcoming summer. Through the window, Alex could see the leaves on the tree were green and bright, the day was similar to the one she had left. Her disused vocal cords cracked as she tried to call out, and pain in her neck indicated that something was protruding from it. A single tube fed oxygen to her nostrils, but an uncomfortable feeling rose from her throat. She felt her neck and found a plastic tube extended from it. The heart rate monitor began to beep, and she looked around at the tubes and electrodes poking from every part of her body. Her panic set off an alarm, and a nurse walked in casually to check. She dropped a tray of small paper cups containing pills which scattered across the ground. Another nurse came running, and together they scrambled about. One of them rushed back out as several more nurses joined them.

"It's okay, Alex. Try to relax." One of the nurses pushed her back down as she struggled against the tubes and needles that seemed to be coming out of her from every direction. She imagined this must have been what Neo felt like when he woke up from the Matrix.

"Have you called Mrs. Henderson yet?" Alex assumed it must be the head nurse.

Alex's eyes darted around the room, and the hospital came to life. As people joined the room, Alex became increasingly panicked. She hadn't been worried until everyone else seemed to be. A gagging feeling spread through her chest as she tried to speak. Someone shone a flashlight in her eyes and told her to look from one wall to the next. Another poked at her feet,

"Do you feel that, sweetie?"

Nod.

"And that?"

Nod.

"Are you going to stay with us this time?"

Nod.

"Are you going to stay with us this time?" They had sat her up and one nurses rubbed Alex's back as she spoke in her ear. It was a cheerful enough question, but Alex didn't feel like talking to anyone. Once they were sure she wasn't going to lapse back into unconsciousness, she was left with only a few nurses attending her. The doctor came in an hour later.

"How long has the patient been active?" Alex watched the doctor move to the end of the bed and pick up her chart without making even the slightest eye contact. The nurse answered his questions as he rattled them off.

"Heartrate Stable?"

"Yes doctor."

"Fluids? I'm assuming she's not eating yet." At that Alex's stomach growled. The mention of food made her realize how hungry she was.

"Mother on the way?"

"She should be here soon."

"Keep me posted." And he walked out without so much as an acknowledgement. Alex wanted to scream at him. So many days she had wished for invisibility, but when it was granted it was infuriating. Did he not realize she was a living breathing person with feelings!

"Nice to see ya back, kid." The nurse seemed to try and compensate as she followed him out of the room. She smiled and squeezed her foot patronizingly.

When Alex's mother arrived, she rushed across the room, squeezing Alex as tightly as she could. "I'm sorry Alex, I'm so sorry."

Alex tried to speak to reassure her mother that it was just as much her fault, but the tube in her throat still prevented her from making any sounds at all. Instead, she just squeezed her mother as tightly as her neglected arms would allow and wept.

###

The summer flew by, and not a day passed when she didn't think of Thomas and her friends in Wonderland. She stared out the window of the bus, wringing her hands, as they approached the school. Most of the other students buzzed with the excitement of a new year. She had missed an entire year while she was in Wonderland.

She had tried to figure out the time differential, but, in the end, concluded that it was simply 'different.' She wondered how much time had passed in Wonderland.

Her mother had taken a position at a smaller firm, giving her more time to spend at home, and her and Alex spent most of their time getting to know each other again. Alex's hand brushed across the scar lefty by the feeding tube. She didn't relish the fuel that Tasha and her gang would have against her when she finally arrived back at school, not to mention that she would be starting in a lower grade than the rest of them.

Alex's mother had offered to Homeschool her, but something had changed in Alex. She no longer wanted to run from her problems. She looked forward to facing them. After all, she had helped vanquish and evil Queen in another world, she was sure she could handle one in this world too.

The bus pulled up to the curb and hissed as the front end lowered to let them out. Alex stepped into the warm fall day, and took a deep breath as she forged forward, head held high. The other kids whispered and pointed at her as she walked by. She noticed the other students looking at her, some of them not even bothering to hide the fact they were pointing at her. She had expected to be the target of attention, though, since most of the school was under the impression that she had jumped in front of the car. The bus stopped and Alex strode across the schoolyard with her head held high.

"Well if it isn't Frankengirl," a female voice came from behind just as she reached the front doors of the school. Alex whirled around, one foot already on the stone steps, and saw Tasha approaching.

"Did they remove the electrodes after they zapped you awake?" one of the boys called from the back of the small group that trailed behind.

"She's even got the scars to prove she's a monster. Careful boys, she'll eat your brains," Tasha finally weighed in, her voice cold, daring Alex to respond. Her following had shrunk since the last time they met, and Tasha only had three other sheep trotting behind her. Alex could see the slight hesitation in her eyes.

"Well…" Alex responded, her own voice surprisingly cool, "we all know who the monsters really were in Frankenstein." Without another word she turned and walked away, shoulders thrown back.

As she walked down the hallway, she began to listen to the whispers of the pointing students.

"She's the one that survived the crash."

"Look at that cool scar!"

"I'm so glad she made it."

These people seemed genuinely happy to see her back at school. They weren't making fun of her at all, and she was mildly shocked that people had missed her.

It didn't take long before the conversations turned to more mundane teenage topics like what happened over summer, and who the new kids were. One conversation was hard not to overhear as the two younger girls stood tittering beside her locker.

"Did you see the new guy?!"

"OH… MY… GOD… yes! He's so cute!" they giggled and laughed and poked each other, daring each other to say hello the next time they saw him.

"Shhhh… here he comes," one of them said.

Alex twisted, mildly interested in finding out who the new center of attention at school might be. Her books dropped out of her hands, crashing to the floor as he rounded the corner. He looked a little older than the last time they had seen each other, but then, she too had aged a whole year in a week. She froze, unsure if it was a doppelganger, but his direction was unwavering as he walked directly up to her, grabbed her in his arms, and kissed her deeply. The voices of the rest of the students stopped as instantly as Alex's breath.

His lips felt warm and soft, her knees gave way, and he held her up as she melted into his arms. She hadn't even realized she had been longing for just that thing. When she recovered from the shock, she returned his embrace and his kiss. She could hear the disappointed protests from the other girls in the hallway, but didn't care. When the kiss ended they simply held each other for a few moments.

"Ready for another adventure?" Thomas whispered.

# ABOUT THE AUTHOR

A lifelong bibliophile and weaver of tales, Lesley Moody has spent over 20 years surrounded by the magic of stories. Her experience as a bookseller and librarian fueled a love for imaginative fiction, culminating in a Bachelor of Arts in Creative Writing and membership in the Imaginative Fiction Writers Association. Now, with "Charred," Lesley takes a fresh look at happily-ever-afters, crafting a science fiction fantasy blend that explores what lies beyond the final page of a beloved fairy tale.

www.ingramcontent.com/pod-product-compliance
Lightning Source LLC
Chambersburg PA
CBHW061231170626
46809CB00007B/2625